Andy
&
Willie

Andy
&
Willie

by Lee Sheridan Cox

Charles Scribner's Sons
New York

To my Mother

CONTENTS

I   Willie Perkins and I Get into the Detective Business   1

II   A Lot of Bad Luck   6

III   Our First Client   11

IV   We Go Detecting   16

V   A Mysterious Payment   23

VI   Making Things Happen   27

VII   A Thief in School   36

VIII   Willie and I Foil a Frame-up   43

IX   Freddie Clark Looks Ahead   49

X   Looking for a Missing Quality   53

XI   A Tricky Plan   57

XII   A Surprise Party   62

XIII   Hubert Gets Out a Special Edition   68

XIV   Ronald Wins a Prize   75

XV   More Bad Luck   81

XVI   A Terrific Deduction   85

XVII   All Tied Up   89

XVIII   An Unbelievable Mystery   95

XIX   Ronald Makes an Accusation   98

XX   Willie and I Make an Accusation   103

XXI   A Hunch and a Prediction   107

XXII	Caught in the Act	112
XXIII	"Blessed Are the Peacemakers"	117
XXIV	A Bloodcurdling Performance	127
XXV	A Strange Disappearance	134
XXVI	A Good Deal of Glory	140
XXVII	A Matter of National Security	146
XXVIII	Candidates and Campaigns	152
XXIX	Trouble at the Polls	161
XXX	A Stake in the Future	167
XXXI	Time to Take a Breather	175

Andy
&
Willie

Chapter I
WILLIE PERKINS AND I GET INTO
THE DETECTIVE BUSINESS

My name is Andy North. I am ten years old going on eleven, and I have lived all my life so far in Wakanda, Indiana. Edgar Bolger, who lives in New York City and spends his summers in Wakanda visiting his grandfather and bragging about New York, says that nobody in New York has ever even heard of Wakanda. This sounds fishy, especially since Edgar also says that New Yorkers are better informed than anybody else. After all, Wakanders have all heard of New York. So, as my best friend Willie Perkins pointed out, how are New Yorkers better informed if they have never heard of Wakanda, which is a well-

1

known town, especially around here? Edgar's claims just don't hang together.

However, in case by a slim chance you haven't heard of Wakanda, I'll describe it, because it's where all of Willie's and my adventures have happened since we went into the detective business. First of all, Wakanda is the ideal, comfortable size. It has a population of three thousand one hundred and twenty-eight, not counting seven people I know personally who were not born in time for the census. Also, though Edgar is always bragging about how much more activity there is in New York City, there is a considerable amount of activity in Wakanda. Mr. McCotter, who spends most of every day sitting on a bench in front of the post office looking at the town, says so. And he says that Wakanda's reputation for being an up-and-coming community dates back several hundred years. For example, according to Mr. McCotter, there was once a woman living here who was scalped, and as Willie said to Edgar, how much more activity would anyone want?

An interesting fact about this scalping, by the way, was that it wasn't fatal. Mr. McCotter says that if an Indian had been converted by missionaries so that he didn't want to do too much damage and if the victim was in good physical condition, a person could survive a scalping. This particular woman was five years old at the time and in good shape. She lived to be fifty-five, and she was bald the last fifty years. At the age of fifty-five she was struck by lightning. Mr. McCotter, who knows all this for a fact, told Willie and me about it to illustrate the advantage of keeping in good physical condition.

Of course, this Indian activity was a long time ago. But it proves that this has been a lively place for years. Even Edgar had to admit that he had never heard of anybody's being scalped in New York City. Also, after he had listened to some of Mr. McCotter's other Indian stories, Edgar even admitted that Wakanda has it all over New York when it comes to an authority on Indians. Mr. McCotter, who is so old that he has a beard clear down to the fourth button on his shirt, is a firsthand authority because when he was a boy, he himself—with his own eyes —saw Indian arrowheads by the dozen all along the creek in Addams' Woods.

Big Walnut Creek, which curves around the south side of town, is another good point about Wakanda. Above the bend in the creek, there is a hole which Mr. McCotter says is probably the most bottomless hole in the Middle West. And below the bend the creek is swell for fishing and boating and swimming and snakes and turtles and almost everything in season. When Mr. McCotter was a boy, Big Walnut Creek froze solid every winter, and a person could skate on it from November to March. I asked him why the creek doesn't freeze like that every winter now, and he said it's the Communists. They are affecting the atmosphere. When I told this news to my father, he told me that I was not to consider Mr. McCotter an international authority, which is peculiar since Mr. McCotter knows almost as much about the Communists as he does about the Indians.

Anyway, this gives some idea of the town where I live. Actually, Wakanda has only one serious drawback, and that is Ronald Pruitt. Ronald, who is always thinking up trouble for Willie and me, is a creep in our class at school. Nobody likes him but teachers. Mr. McCotter says that Ronald comes from a long line of creeps. And since Ronald's brother Bertie is one, too, it's obvious that creeps run in the family. But aside from them, Wakanda is an ideal place. And it has been getting even more ideal since Willie and I got into the detective business.

Willie and I became detectives last September several weeks after school started. The way it came about was this. Miss Easter, our fifth grade teacher, was enthusiastic about having her students give speeches, and so right away we all had to give a speech on an interesting experience during the summer vacation. I gave a talk which Miss Easter praised for two minutes and fifty-seven seconds. I know this for a fact because Willie, who is quite scientific, timed her. It was the longest anyone was praised. Ronald Pruitt was praised for one minute and three seconds. So Ronald, who has never been able to adjust to the fact that I can beat him at everything, was jealous, and he went around telling everybody that he was going to show me up in the second speech, which we were supposed to give on what we were going to be when we grew up.

I had always planned on being a baseball player like Mickey Mantle or a football player like Johnny Unitas, but when I heard that Ronald was going to talk on being an astronaut, I realized that I had to come up with a more unusual profession. Most of the guys were planning on being athletes—even Jackie Carr, who can't chin himself. Willie told everybody that he was going to be a genius, but he was kidding. He was really at that time planning on being a teacher—a coach, that is. Well, I thought and I thought, and I couldn't figure out anything to beat an astronaut, which, by the way, Ronald couldn't be in a million years because no one would get into a confined space with him. Then the night before the speech was due, I was watching *Big City Detective* on television, and I got to thinking that private eyes have unusually interesting lives. They are always being ambushed, and having knives thrown at them from dark alleys, and getting guns stuck in their backs, and going around corners in foreign cars on two wheels. They get into a lot of fights and meet a lot of interesting people. Besides that, they do good.

So that's what I gave my speech on, and as it turned out, the class liked my speech better than Ronald's. It had a snappy ending. Ronald had been doing this loud, noticeable yawning all the time I talked, and so finally I said, "If Ronald Pruitt gets a black eye on the way home from school this afternoon, and he probably will——"

Ronald shut his mouth, but Miss Easter started to open hers. So I said quickly, "What I mean is, it is sometimes the duty of the detective to give a black eye to a worthless person in the interest of justice. But on the other hand, if even a worthless person is killed, then he's worth something, and the detective goes after the criminal. So I'm going to be a private eye to make the world a better place for the little guy as well as the big guy, or even a creep like Ronald."

Miss Easter started to say that was enough, but I was through anyway.

When the bell rang, Ronald said, "Deadeye North. The private deadeye. You couldn't follow a cow's trail."

I winked at Willie, and Willie said, "Write us a letter about it from Mars, why don't you?"

Right away, Willie had decided to be a detective, too. He said that finding stolen jewels was a lot better than just getting into games free, which is all that happens to a coach, besides having a whole town down on you if five other guys lose a basketball game. And Willie talks a lot. After we had decided to study up to be detectives, he kept telling everybody what we were doing, and Ronald kept making wisecracks, and almost before we knew it, we found ourselves right in the middle of the detective business.

Chapter II
A LOT OF BAD LUCK

What we were doing which Willie kept talking about to everybody—first we went to the library and found a book on judo. If someone is waiting around a corner to stick a knife in you, you've got to be able to protect yourself. Willie is little, and after I'd thrown him around the room a few times he got discouraged. He said that until the Wheaties started taking hold, maybe he wasn't built for the detective business. But I pointed out that he was a good size to sneak through a tight place like a transom, and so he brightened up and decided to give the judo another try.

Willie got quite good at the bow and the yell, and I got good at throwing him in every direction, but finally he quit cooperating because he said he thought I'd broken one or two small bones in his back. We had to quit anyway because we'd also broken a vase and some other odds and ends of my mother's, and she said that she was getting in the mood for a little judo herself.

Besides, my father said that this was enough of this nonsense. So we took the book on judo back and found one on the FBI which told all about fingerprinting. But my mother said what were all the smudges on the wall in the bathroom. I explained that we were studying our fingerprints. I told her how you had to study them and read what the book said so you'd recognize things about them and know whose they were. She said if Willie and I didn't stop leaving them around, she'd fingerprint us both. My father said he thought he'd said that this was enough of this nonsense.

It's hard to amount to anything when you've got parents to buck all the time, but Willie and I weren't giving up. We decided to practice shadowing people. I shadowed my father a couple of times and got pretty good at moving from tree to tree. I also worked on entering a room without anybody's knowing I was there. But once before dinner when I'd slipped into the kitchen and was keeping an eye on my mother in case she did something suspicious, I all of a sudden wondered what we were having for dinner, and when I just asked, my mother dropped a bowl of batter and had a nervous breakdown. She told my father that I kept creeping around. My father said just one more thing and I would have the sorest bottomside of any detective in Wakanda.

At this point we would probably have given up being

detectives if it hadn't been for Ronald Pruitt's wisecracks. And he had told his brother Bertie about Willie and me training for the detective business. If there's a bigger creep in the world than Ronald, it's Bertie. Being fifteen, he's had five years more practice.

"Hey, Eyes," he'd yell at Willie and me, "put the finger on anyone yet?"

One time downtown, with a lot of people around, Bertie yelled at Willie, "There's the great detective, Dupin Perkins. Anybody been purloined lately, Dupin?"

Willie said it was embarrassing to have something peculiar like that yelled at him so everybody could hear it. And Willie got so fed up that finally one day at school during recess when Ronald was sneering around and asking when we thought we'd be hired for our first case, Willie forgot everything except getting back at Ronald.

"We're already working on a case," said Willie.

"I don't believe it," said Ronald. "Who would hire you?"

"I'm not going to tell our client's name," said Willie. "It isn't ethical."

"You're not telling because there's nothing to tell," said Ronald.

"What makes you an authority?" said Archie Monroe.

"I'm not a moron," said Ronald. "Anybody who believes that Willie and Andy are really on a case is a moron."

"Oh, go soak your head," said Freddie Clark.

Ronald isn't what you'd call popular.

"We are, aren't we, Andy?" said Willie, who was looking sweaty.

8

"Yes," I said. I couldn't let Willie down.

"And we'll be paid a lot of money when we break the case, which should be any day now," said Willie.

"We can't give out any more information," I said.

So then Willie acted so mysterious that all the kids, except Ronald, believed we really were on a case. After school, Willie said he'd almost got to believing it himself, which ought to be good for business.

That evening I was carrying home some groceries and thinking how Willie had stuck our necks out when I saw Bertie sitting on his bike in front of Antonelli's Candy Kitchen. I almost turned and went around the block, but I didn't.

"Well, if it isn't Sherlock out on a case," he said when he saw me, "and Watson. Sherlock, you'd better get out your magnifying glass because it looks as if Watson's got a clue."

I turned to see what he was looking at, and there was my dog G. C. sniffing at the sidewalk. I call him Garbage Can—G. C. for short. He's a good little old dog, and he was minding his own business, and so I got mad. I won't stand for anybody's calling Garbage Can names.

"His name is G. C.," I said. "You'd better not call him that again."

"W'at son?" said Bertie, and the guys hanging around laughed.

A person can take only so much. I lowered my head and ran at Bertie and butted him in the side so hard that he lost his balance and the handlebars of his bike slammed against the window and cracked it. So out came Mr. Antonelli, who is usually big and fat and friendly, but who at this point was looking big and fat and unfriendly.

"Andy did it," said Bertie. "It's his fault. He knocked me over."

"Accept my condolences," said Mr. Antonelli. "Now do you want to pay me four dollars, which is half the cost of the glass, and leave and not come back until you learn how to behave in public, or do you want me to tell your father about all the trouble you keep having with people who are half your size?"

Mr. Antonelli can get tough, as everybody knows. And Bertie didn't waste any time paying and leaving. Since I sicked G. C. on him under my breath, Bertie didn't leave alone. All people like Bertie Pruitt should always leave chased by dogs. It calls attention to their meanness.

So then Mr. Antonelli turned to me and said, "You'll have to pay the other half, Andy. I'll settle it with your father."

"Couldn't you settle it with me?" I said.

"You don't need to look so frightened," said Mr. Antonelli in a more friendly tone. "I saw only the last part of what happened, but I'll tell your father that I know enough of Bertie to guess that he started the whole thing. You shouldn't go around breaking windows though."

"I'm sorry Bertie hit your window," I said. "If I had it to do over again, I'd try to knock him in a different direction."

"That isn't exactly what I had in mind," said Mr. Antonelli. "At any rate, now you have a window to pay for."

"I know it," I said. "And I'll pay for it myself. I can pay you thirty cents now and the rest in a week. I don't like to bother my father with this. He has several other things on his mind."

Mr. Antonelli considered the matter for a while. Finally he said, "All right. I'll give you one week. But just one week and no excuses."

I started home wishing that Ronald and Bertie were tied to a railroad track with a train coming. All I had at home, plus my allowance at the end of the week added up to just eighty-seven cents. I didn't know where I was going to get the $2.83. But I had to get it because there is a way my father has of saying "one more thing" which really means "one more thing." I wished I'd never heard of the detective business.

Chapter III
OUR FIRST CLIENT

I was so depressed that I didn't hear Tim O'Brien until he caught up with me and said he'd been yelling at me for a block. Tim is an important person in Wakanda. He is the best sophomore basketball player in school and the quarterback on the high school football team. The only thing wrong with him is that he lets Polly Merrill order him around, which is peculiar since he can throw a discus two hundred feet. Polly is my cousin who always has a lot of boys calling her on the telephone and hanging around her house getting on my uncle's nerves. My uncle,

11

who may not realize that Tim has the best backhand of any tennis player in town, is the only person I know who does not admire Tim. I personally heard him call Tim an idiot's idiot. But then the only good thing I ever heard him say about any of Polly's friends was that the more he saw of the voters of the future, the more faith he put in the motto, "In God We Trust."

"I just heard that you have a bill to pay," said Tim. "I've got an idea. Do you want a job?"

"What kind of job?" I said.

"You want to be a detective, don't you?" said Tim.

"You think you're funny," I said and started home with my groceries. I was depressed enough without having to hear Tim O'Brien, who can run a mile in four minutes and five seconds, talk like that creep Bertie.

He kept telling me that he was on the level, but I wouldn't pay any attention until he said, "Andy, I'll tell you what the job is. Polly has a certain letter in her possession. You get it, and I'll pay you whatever your charge on a case is."

This didn't sound like kidding. "Whose letter is it?" I said.

"It's mine. I wrote it to her."

"Then it's hers, isn't it?" I said.

"Well, technically," said Tim.

"I'm not stealing for anybody," I said. "It's against the law."

"But your cousin Polly is blackmailing me with that letter," said Tim. "Now what does a detective do when he's hired by someone who is being blackmailed? He gets the damaging evidence back, doesn't he? That's not stealing. What's your fee?"

"Three dollars," I said. "But I don't want the job. It sounds funny."

"For Pete's sake, Andy, do you think I'd ask you to do anything really dishonest?" said Tim. "Actually, Polly is the one who is breaking the law. I tell you she's blackmailing me. I'm in a real jam, and you're practically my last hope."

This put a new light on things. "I'm not saying we'll take the case," I said, "but how would Willie and I recognize this letter if we saw it?"

"Polly is keeping it in a long blue envelope with no stamp on it and with some writing in red pencil in the upper right hand corner. I know, because she has been waving it at me across the study hall all day. Since you are her cousin, you can prowl around in her house without attracting attention. The letter is probably in her school notebook. At least, that's where she was keeping it today. You get it by Friday, and I'll pay you three dollars."

"Why is it so valuable?" I said.

Tim said I didn't need to know. But I said that Willie and I definitely could not take the case then. So he made me swear that we wouldn't tell, and then he told me this dull story.

He said that he had always preferred Polly to all the other girls and that he'd thought that she preferred him to all the other guys, though he'd always known that the other guys all preferred Polly, too, and that most of them thought she preferred them.

13

"Any more *preferreds* and I'm going to lose track of what's going on," I said.

"OK," said Tim. "In short, I thought Polly had a sincere regard for me."

"Anybody can see that you are the best athlete in town," I said.

"That's not what I mean," said Tim. "But skip it. Anyway, last summer, when I was at the lake with my family, I got a letter from her, and she happened to mention that she'd heard that I was dating Connie Smith, who was there at the lake, too. Naturally, I was surprised."

"I should think so," I said. It surprised me to hear that Polly would bother to send such dumb, unnecessary news clear across the state.

"As far as I was concerned, Connie wasn't even there. So I wrote Polly that somebody was misinformed. And I threw in a few items about Connie's personality and appearance—things which weren't true, but just to make sure that Polly hadn't got the wrong impression."

It was unbelievable. Here was the best athlete in town wasting his vacation writing untrue letters about one girl to another girl when he could have been in swimming, and then saying he did it to keep somebody from getting the wrong impression.

"I was a victim of circumstance," said Tim. "Anyway, a few days later I happened to be sitting on Connie's porch when the mail came and she got a letter from Polly. So Connie said, 'Let's see what's happening at home.' But then she read a little to herself, looked embarrassed, said, 'There's nothing much happening,' and put the letter away."

"Doesn't anything happen in this story?" I said.

"Right away, Connie's manner made me suspect that there was something in that letter that she was hiding from me. But she is such a good friend of Polly's that I couldn't get her to tell me what it was. However, as time went by, I figured out from little things she started to say before she stopped herself that Polly makes fun of everybody, especially me, and that people were surprised that a person like me would let Polly pull the wool over his eyes. At first, I felt low. But Connie was always there to cheer me up. And I began to realize that she is well-named—Constancy, that is. So I started dating her after all, because a guy admires a girl who is sincere."

"What's all this got to do with blackmail?" I said.

"That letter about Connie being goofy, squinteyed, et cetera," said Tim. "I'd forgotten it. Then last week Polly phoned me and said that if I don't take her to the fall mixer Friday night, she'll show Connie the letter. And naturally Connie thinks I'll take *her*. I don't know what to do. Every time I try to reason with Polly, she quotes from that crazy letter."

"Is this the only way she can get to the dance?" I said.

"All the guys would like to take Polly," said Tim. "But she's made a bet that I will take her, instead of Connie, to the dance. She's just interested in winning a bet. Andy, you've got to try to get that letter."

We had reached my house. I thought about what would happen if I couldn't pay Mr. Antonelli and he told my father that I had broken a window. Then I thought about that creep Ronald Pruitt. I looked at Tim, and he reminded me of G. C. in the rain.

15

"We'll take the case," I said.

As I went into my house, I saw Polly, who lives next door to me, looking through the window at Tim and me. I have always liked Polly, and when she waved to me, I felt guilty. But then I remembered that she was a blackmailer.

Chapter IV
WE GO DETECTING

That evening Willie and I sneaked around Polly's house and worked along on our stomachs behind the shrubbery until we were by the front porch where Polly and some other girls were talking. After about fifteen minutes Willie started backing away. So I crawled after him, and when we reached the back of the house, he got up and started scratching himself.

"I've got bugs all over me," he said, "and I can't stand that dopey talk one more minute."

"We might get a clue any time," I said. "They've mentioned Tim eight times already."

"And thirty-six other guys," said Willie. "I don't think that this is the way to go about it. I think we should ask to use the bathroom and then go to Polly's room and search it while she's on the porch."

"If they don't know you're there, you've got to have a search warrant," I said.

Willie said he was just as up on the detective business as I was and he was going to detect in his own way.

We had an argument which took quite a while, and then we had a fight which didn't take long. So Willie agreed to go listen for a clue, since it was more scientific.

When we crawled back, three boys, including Bertie Pruitt, were on the porch.

"Why do you think Tim will take you?" Bertie was saying. "What makes you so sure?"

"I'm not sure," said Polly. "In fact, there's a reason that makes me almost hope he won't."

"What reason?" said Bertie. "So I'll win the bet and you'll be sworn to give me six dances at the next three mixers?"

"Hardly, Repulsive," said Polly.

"What if you win, Polly?" somebody said.

"Bertie does my math for two months and doesn't talk to me for two weeks."

There was a lot of laughter.

"But I can't lose," said Bertie. "This is one time when Polly won't win. Tim keeps saying that sincerity and dependability are the traits to look for. and he says that Connie's got them."

"Connie is dependable, all right," said Polly. "You can always depend on her for something devious. She wrote me last summer that Tim was giving her a big rush, which wasn't true, and then when that didn't work she——"

Right here Willie sneezed. It was sort of a yell and a sneeze mixed together, and it was so loud and sudden that everybody jumped about eight inches up. Willie ran, but before I could get away, Bertie had grabbed me and was dragging me up onto the porch.

17

"Well, if it isn't Nero Wolfe," he said, digging his fingers into my arm muscle.

"My goodness, Andy," said Polly, "what are you doing down there?"

"We are collecting bugs," I said, which certainly was true.

"They are eavesdropping," said Bertie. "Working on a case, Hawkshaw?" he said, shoving me around. "Broken any windows lately?"

"Bertie, you are the worst bully I ever saw," said Polly. "Leave him alone. Stop pushing him. Andy can collect bugs in my bushes any time he likes."

All the girls started bawling Bertie out for being mean to little children. Bertie was trying to tell about Willie's and my detective ambitions and trying to say that we *were* eavesdropping, but his hold on me loosened, and so I jerked away and ran. I kicked him first. Willie was waiting behind the house. He said he hadn't planned to sneeze. He said that he thought a bug got in his nose.

"It's all right," I said. "Except if Bertie succeeds in making Polly suspicious of us, it'll be twice as hard to find the letter."

"Well, if we don't find it," said Willie, "Tim will probably have to take Polly to the dance, and Bertie will lose the bet. And I don't want to help Bertie to win anything."

Personally, I agreed with Willie. But I told him it was as I'd said in my speech in class. Private eyes can't have private feelings, and besides, Polly was breaking the law, and besides, we'd promised Tim to take the case.

"And besides, you need the three bucks," said Willie.

So we went down the alley to the next block and cut

across the street and then came back to a spot across the street from Polly's house. Bertie and the rest were leaving.

"Aren't you coming, Polly?" someone said. "I thought it was your idea to go to Antonelli's."

"There's something I want to do first," said Polly. "You go ahead. I'll catch up with you."

We sneaked across the street after Polly's friends were gone and looked through Polly's living room windows. I thought afterwards how lucky we were. First, Willie kept doing so much unnecessary talking that it's a wonder somebody didn't hear him.

"This is what you call casing the joint," he said, which I already knew. "Boy, my mom would kill me," he said, which I already knew.

Then when Polly came into the room, he kicked me to be sure I noticed what she was carrying and caught me right behind my left knee so that I fell against the house and made a terrible racket. But we were really lucky. Polly didn't hear us even when G. C. turned up unexpectedly and started barking and we had to grab him and hold him down and clamp his mouth shut. It was close quarters between the shrubbery and the windows, and old G. C.'s tail kept slapping against the house, but apparently Polly was thinking so hard about where to hide the long, blue envelope in her hand that she didn't hear a thing. She stood for a while right by the window, tapping the envelope against her chin and looking around the room. Then she walked over to a table by the door, hid the envelope under some magazines on it, called to her mother that she would be back in an hour, and left. Up to then we were really lucky.

I was just starting to go into the house for the envelope when Polly's mother came into the room and sat down by the table where the magazines were.

"Well, good night," said Willie. "Now what do we do?"

"This is easy," I said. "You wait here. I'll go home and phone and say their dog is bothering somebody. While my aunt is explaining that they don't have a dog, you hop inside and get the letter."

So I was holding my nose, waiting to talk to my aunt, when who should answer the telephone but my uncle. I was so surprised that I said, "Uncle Fred?"

"Hello, Andy," he said.

I couldn't think of anything to say, and so I said, "Are you at home?"

"Where else would I be answering my telephone?" he said. "What can I do for you, Andy?"

"Excuse me. I seem to have the wrong number," I said and hung up.

I rejoined Willie at the window, and my uncle came into the room shaking out a newspaper as if he were mad at it. He'd been doing some yelling Willie said. My uncle yells around a lot, especially about the telephone. So he sat down and began to read, and now there were two people sitting by the letter, both of them looking as if they were settled there for the next hundred years.

We decided that the only thing we could do was to go calling and look for a chance to grab that envelope when nobody was looking. So we knocked at the door, and I said I had come to apologize to Uncle Fred for having the wrong number. So I apologized and my uncle rattled his newspaper and then Willie and I sat down. While Willie and my aunt were making conversation, I tried to figure out how a detective would go about getting that letter. My aunt was the one to worry about because my uncle was down behind the newspaper in the financial page.

All of a sudden I got an idea. Whenever I'm at my aunt's and I need a drink of water, she usually goes with me to help me out. So to get her away from the letter, I asked whether I could have a drink. But this time she told me to help myself, that I knew where the glasses were. I got up, giving Willie a look which he misunderstood. He said that he'd like to have a drink, too. My aunt told him to go along with me, but I gave him another look. So he said that on second thought he didn't want one. My uncle rattled his newspaper.

When I got to the kitchen, I called to my aunt to ask her about the glasses until finally she came to help me. I took plenty of time drinking, and when we went back to the living room, I saw by the look on Willie's face that he had the letter. So I thanked my aunt for the water, and we left.

"Good for you, Willie," I said when we got away from the house and he pulled the letter out from under his shirt. "That's what I call real detecting."

"I almost had a heart attack," said Willie. "I'd just got over to the table and was starting to look through the magazines when your uncle lowered his newspaper and focused on me. He's got an eye like a barracuda. He finally began to read again, but boy, this detective business is hard on the nerves."

We took the letter straight over to Tim's house.

At first Tim acted as if he couldn't believe it. Then he kept yelling, "It's it! Zowie!"

"How about the three dollars?" I said.

"Just a minute," said Tim. "I'll get it."

He ran up the stairs.

"I guess our first case was a success," said Willie. "I guess this'll show Ronald Pruitt."

"I don't feel so good about it," I said. "Now Bertie will win the bet."

Then Tim yelled. He sounded as if he had been ambushed. "Andy!" he shouted. "Willie!" He came down the steps three at a time. "You've got to put this back. Quick. Before Polly misses it. Or does she know now?"

"No," I said. "But she said that she'd be home in an hour about an hour ago."

"Is it the wrong letter?" said Willie.

"No," said Tim. "Yes. No. Can you get it back without Polly's knowing? I'll still pay the three dollars."

I said that we could try, and the next minute Tim was rushing us out to his car and driving off practically before we were inside. We reached Polly's house in three minutes. Tim went around the last corner on two wheels. It was the time I felt most like a detective.

Chapter V
A MYSTERIOUS PAYMENT

When we got there, there was no sign of Polly. Tim shoved the envelope at me and told me in a hoarse voice to hurry. He said that if he saw Polly coming, he would warn me by honking his horn. I didn't have any pockets big enough to hide the envelope, and so I stuck it inside the front of my pants, and then Willie and I went up on the porch and knocked. My aunt was surprised to see us again.

"Excuse me for bothering you," I said, "but perhaps I left my magazine here."

"What kind of magazine, Andy?" she said.

"Maybe he laid it there on the table," said Willie.

We went to the table with my aunt asking a lot of questions and going through the magazines. Then the horn began to honk out in front, and I discovered that the letter had slipped down to where I couldn't get hold of it without attracting attention.

"Could I have a drink?" I said.

"Great Scot," said my uncle.

I hurried to the kitchen and got the letter out. Then I hurried back, holding it behind me, and Willie, who is fast in an emergency, handed me a couple of magazines. I slipped the letter between them and laid them back on the table. All the time the horn kept honking, and my uncle said, "What idiot is sounding that horn?"

"I believe I remember where I left the magazine," I said. "It wasn't here."

"It's at your house, isn't it?" said Willie. "Yessir, I remember too."

My uncle looked sort of swollen, and so we said goodbye in a hurry.

When we went out onto the porch, we heard Polly saying, "Why, Tim, is that you?"

"It's this crazy horn," said Tim. "Sometimes I have to stop to fix it. While I'm here though, Polly, since I just happen to be here, I'd like to take the opportunity to ask you to go to the dance with me Friday night, and I don't mean because of the letter but because I want you to."

Willie and I tried to figure it out on the way home.

"I like the way it turned out," said Willie, "but how did it get that way? We're the detectives. Aren't we supposed to know?"

I had to admit that I didn't understand it either. On the playground before school the next morning we were still trying to make some sense out of what had happened when along came Tim waving three dollar bills over his head and calling, "Andy North! Willie Perkins!" He looked very cheerful. Of course, a lot of kids, including Ronald Pruitt, gathered around to see what was going on.

"Here's the fee," said Tim, "for a job well done."

"A detective job," said Willie to all the kids.

You should have seen Ronald's face. He looked as if he'd just seen an abnormal alien from outer space.

"Just one thing," said Tim, taking Willie and me

to one side. "Remember, Polly must never know what I hired you to do. So don't tell anyone."

"Why not?" I said. "How're we going to build up a reputation unless people know all about our cases?"

"The situation is changed," said Tim. "You can't tell it."

"But it's all over," said Willie. "Detectives always tell everything when it's over."

"Not necessarily," said Tim. "In this situation publicity would spoil all the good work you've done."

"I don't see why," I said.

"I'll tell you," said Tim finally, "if you'll promise to keep the explanation under your hat."

We told him that he could count on us. So then he said, "The letter about Connie was in the envelope all right, but an unfinished letter that Polly was writing to her sister happened to be with it. I took out the wrong letter by mistake and saw what it said before I realized what it was."

"But she was blackmailing you," I said. "After all, you didn't intend to read the wrong letter, and you had us put it right back."

"You don't get it," said Tim. "I had you put them *both* back. Polly was telling her sister how I had let Connie Smith poison my mind against her. She said I had such high ideals that I never recognized sneakiness in others since I never did anything underhanded myself. So you can imagine how I felt standing there with a letter I'd stolen."

"Stolen?" I said.

"From her point of view," said Tim. "Because

she wasn't trying to blackmail me. She was trying to save me from that squint-eyed Connie Smith. She thinks that I just suddenly realized that Connie poisoned my mind. If she knew that I hired you to get the letter, she'd lose her good opinion of me. So you can't tell it."

We agreed, and so everything ended up fine. I paid Mr. Antonelli that evening. He said I was a good boy and he wouldn't tell my father about the window, which he hasn't to this day. And Ronald was so stunned at Willie's and my success that he could hardly talk for a while.

But something happened the next day that stunned even Willie and me. We were on the playground at noon, and we heard somebody calling us. It was Polly. She looked very cheerful. All the kids gathered around to see what was going on.

"How much is it you charge for a case?" said Polly.

"Three dollars," I said.

"Very reasonable," she said, handed me three dollars, and walked away.

Since everybody was looking on, Willie and I pulled ourselves together and acted nonchalant, as if getting paid for solving a case was getting to be old stuff. But that evening we went to tell Polly that she must have made a mistake. She just laughed. When we tried to give the money back, she got very bossy and wouldn't take it.

Willie thinks she's not all there. I thought at first that maybe she'd discovered that Willie and I had indirectly helped her to win the bet from Bertie. But that didn't make sense, because then she'd be angry with Tim for doing something underhanded from her point of view. And naturally she'd be mad at us, too, for helping him.

So what was she paying us for? We considered investigating the whole matter since the payment was so mysterious and it is Willie's and my job to solve mysteries. But Mr. McCotter said that investigating the mind of a female could discourage the best detectives in the world. So Willie and I decided to leave it a mystery. We didn't want to get discouraged right at the beginning of a big career.

Chapter VI
MAKING THINGS HAPPEN

Ronald Pruitt is the kind of person that if a teacher wants to send a note to another teacher she picks Ronald to deliver it. He is also the type who not only reads the note but looks in everybody's locker on the way down the hall. In short, as I have pointed out before, Ronald is a born creep. He also works at it. He plots and he waits and he never gives up. And the minute a person makes a mistake, Ronald is ready to take advantage of it. I keep telling Willie that having Ronald to guard against all our lives has really been a good thing because it has toughened us up and prepared us for the detective business. But sometimes it is hard to look on the bright side.

For example, after Willie and I were paid twice right in front of everybody for solving a case, Ronald stopped making wisecracks about detectives. You'd have thought that he was squelched for good, but then something happened which showed that he was just biding his time. We were having this dull recitation in class on the main exports of the United States, and for relief I got to thinking about lassoing a sucker. I'd never been able to lasso one, but Mr. McCotter had told me how it was done and had said that if I imagined the process often enough in my spare time, the time would come when I could really do it. So I started imagining. I pretended that I was lying on a certain tree limb that juts way out over Big Walnut Creek. The water was clear and clean the way it is in April, and I could see a whole bunch of suckers swimming along in the water below me. I tossed a little rock into the water, and a big sucker turned around and came back to investigate. I was dangling a line with copper wire and a noose on the end into the water, and very carefully, as the sucker came swimming along, I let the noose go easy over his head. Then I gave a quick jerk on the line. Unfortunately, I was so carried away at the prospect of catching this sucker, which was the biggest one I'd ever seen, that I jerked myself clear out of my seat in class and onto the floor. Miss Easter, who happened to be looking at me at the time, had a harder time getting over it than I did. She was so upset that she almost sent for the school nurse. She thought I was having a fit.

This is the kind of accident that Ronald waits for and is always prepared to take advantage of. At recess he told everybody that I was defective, which made me a defective detective. He probably got this from Bertie, who had probably read it somewhere, and Ronald had probably just been waiting for an opportunity to use it. I will admit that it's funny, but it wasn't funny to hear people laugh and to have to hear the same remark about a million times during the following week. However, a person should never stop looking on the bright side because, although I didn't know it at the time, Willie's and my second big case was coming up, Willie and I were going to fix Ronald, and I was going to prove that I was not a defective detective.

Actually, after being paid three dollars twice in front of everybody, Willie and I had already been hired for several minor jobs. We located missing articles: Jackie Carr's Boy Scout knife, which it turned out Jackie's little sister had sold to Freddie Clark for two cents; Jackie Carr's baseball glove, which it turned out his little sister had sold to Freddie Clark for fifteen cents; Jackie Carr's bicycle, which it turned out his little sister had sold to Freddie Clark for sixty-three cents; Jackie Carr's little sister, who it turned out was supposed to be under Jackie's protection, only Jackie forgot about her until time for his mother to return home. We found her sitting in front of the doctor's office with dark glasses and a cup and a sign saying, "Help the blind." She had seventeen cents in the cup.

Jackie was not only our next client after Tim. He was our next fifteen. He said that a detective agency was exactly what Wakanda needed, and it got so that he was calling us all the time to locate something, but then he always charged it because Jackie is always bankrupt. So Willie and I went to see my Aunt Gertrude, who needs a detective more than anyone else we could think of except Jackie, and she gave us the job of finding her eyeglasses which she had mislaid and couldn't see to find. Willie located them right away. He sat down on a low table to think over where they might be, and there they were under him. You find out a lot about human nature in the detective business. Aunt Gertrude didn't even offer to pay us after we had found her glasses. Willie said the way she carried on about a little crack you could hardly notice in one lens, you'd have thought he sat on her eyeball.

We had counted on a lot of business after our first case was so successful, and so you can see how disappointing it was to have bankrupts like Jackie and welshers like Aunt Gertrude for our only clients. Also, it was discouraging not to have any crime around. We couldn't remember anybody ever being even close to murdered—except maybe Willie and me by our fathers that time we found the keys in Willie's father's car and drove halfway around the block before Aunt Gertrude came along taking up all the road.

And then, right when everything was blackest, Homer XVIII, Willie's frog, got loose and started our second big case. Willie almost always has a frog on him. He kept Homer in his desk at school, and at recess on this particular day when he was taking Homer out for a breath of fresh air, Homer got away behind a table and a filing cabinet in the back of the room.

Willie told me about it later. He was under the table trying to reach Homer when Miss Easter and Miss Crocker, another teacher, came into the room. They didn't see Willie, and naturally he kept quiet because the day he lifted the lid on his desk and Homer unexpectedly jumped on Betsy Miller, Miss Easter had taken Betsy's part instead of Homer's, which was really a surprise. I mean, Miss Easter wore eyeglasses that had a butterfly in jewels on one corner of the frame. Willie had checked on the name of the butterfly in a scientific book, and as he said, you'd think that anybody who would go around all the time with a male Io up over one eye would be fond of wildlife. But she had told Willie very definitely to leave Homer at home. This was impossible. Willie's mother is against frogs.

So Willie kept quiet, waiting for Miss Easter and Miss Crockett to leave, and he couldn't help overhearing this conversation about Mr. Barrie. As everybody knows, Mr. Barrie was always talking to Miss Easter in the hall and coming into her room on errands. He got his own class taught and spent a lot of time in our room, too, which shows how much the taxpayers were getting for their money out of Mr. Barrie. Also, unlike some teachers I could mention, he is a teacher who tells you about important things. For instance, one day he brought in a praying mantis, which he said ate flies. Freddie Clark offered him some dead ones which he happened to have wrapped up in paper in his desk. Freddie is very saving. But Miss Easter, instead of being pleased with Freddie's foresight as Mr. Barrie was, made Freddie clean out his desk, and then as an afterthought, made Willie clean his, too. That's the kind of person Miss Easter is. She's the best-looking teacher we ever had, but she's crazy about desk inspection. And she wasn't as nice to Mr. Barrie as he was to her, which was peculiar since he was my pick of the two.

Anyway, in this conversation Miss Easter was criticizing Mr. Barrie and praising Tod Ayres, a creep who works in his father's bank and chases girls. Actually, except for owning a Jaguar, Tod Ayres can't hold a candle to Mr. Barrie, who owns a 1952 Ford. But Willie said that Miss Easter couldn't find anything good to say about Mr. Barrie except that he was insufferable. Willie, who can get things mixed-up at times, said that it seemed to him that Miss

31

Easter was annoyed because Mr. Barrie wasn't annoyed when she became friendly with Tod Ayres. Willie admitted that this didn't make sense, but he said that none of the conversation hung together much, although they kept using the same words over and over, like *men* and *husbands*. The only thing that was absolutely clear, Willie said, was that Miss Easter hated Mr. Barrie because he didn't know his own mind.

Willie said that Miss Easter really looked down on men who didn't know their own minds. And she said that the men who got ahead in the world were the ones who made things happen, not those who just waited for something to happen. Willie was relieved when they left the room and he could crawl out from under the table with Homer XVIII. He said it was a punk recess, all things considered.

But that afternoon, when we were going home from school, I got to thinking about Miss Easter's saying that a person should make things happen, instead of just waiting for them to happen.

"You know," I said to Willie, "I think she's got something there. If we could just figure out how to start a case that would get everybody's attention, then we could solve it and build up our reputation."

I was remembering something I read once where somebody sent a letter to a lot of people saying, "All is discovered. Get out of town." And I was thinking that if we sent such a letter to the most suspicious people in town, then when they left, we could work on why. I didn't tell Willie about my idea though, because Willie is the type that always wants to get started, and I thought that the idea needed some thinking over. But the next morning during recess Willie came up to me looking as if he'd just won the Kentucky Derby.

"I got it," he said, "about making things happen. It came to me just like that. Come on around here."

We went around to the back of the school building where we had found a loose brick which we could pull out and have a little place to keep items we might need at any minute like water pistols. Willie looked over his shoulder like the government employee in the television series, *I Was a British Traitor,* and then jerked out the brick. I almost died. I'd have recognized that male Io anywhere.

"Miss Easter's glasses!" I said.

"That was a great idea of yours," said Willie.

"My idea!" I said. "I'm for law and order."

"Sure we are," said Willie. "And now we can prove it. It came to me like a flash. Just now I was sneaking back into the classroom to get Homer, and there were Miss Easter's glasses lying on her desk, and I remembered what a racket Aunt Gertrude made about hers and yet how it wouldn't be stealing to take them because who would want anyone else's glasses? So now we find Miss Easter's glasses for her and build up our reputation just as you said."

Well, I could see it from Willie's point of view. But then I got to seeing it from my father's point of view. Willie said that Miss Easter herself would approve because basically it was her own idea. But I said if Willie's father ever found out about it, what would his basic idea be, and he was twice as big as Miss Easter. So then Willie got to

33

seeing it from his father's point of view, and we decided to put the glasses back.

We didn't get a chance. I had them in my pocket ready to put them on her desk when we went in from recess, but I couldn't get near it. Miss Easter was opening and shutting her desk drawers and looking under and behind everything on her desk. And Miss Crockett was running around looking on all the book shelves and tables and filing cabinets. I was getting so nervous that it was a big relief when Miss Easter gave up the search for the time being and started on geography recitation. Without glasses, Miss Easter's eyes aren't worth a nickel. She had Hubert Welsh point out the Euphrates River on the map, and when he pointed at the Nile River, she said, "Very good." I think that she was afraid we would find out she couldn't see us very well, because she kept telling Jackie Carr to pay attention, which is usually a safe thing to say. But once he was. And Ronald Pruitt looked cross-eyed four times when he recited, and you could tell that she didn't know it. At least, ordinarily I think she would have asked him whether he was getting ready to pass out.

I didn't get a chance to put the glasses back in the afternoon either, and having them in my pocket was hard on my nerves. After lunch, Miss Easter asked the class whether anyone knew where her glasses might be, and I almost died when Willie held his hand up. But he just suggested that maybe she had laid them on the window sill and they had fallen out into the bushes. Miss Easter was trying everything by that time, and so she sent Willie out to look, and he looked all through history lesson. Willie isn't interested in history because it's all over. Besides, he wasn't as worried

34

as I was, since the glasses weren't making a bulge in his pocket.

But I had heard that there was going to be a teachers' meeting after school. So after they marched us out that afternoon, Willie and I waited for about fifteen minutes and then sneaked back into the building. We could hear the principal going on about something up in the room where they hold meetings to discuss us, but we peeped around Miss Easter's door to be sure that the coast was clear. And who should be washing the blackboard but that creep Ronald Pruitt. Ronald is always doing this to get in good with the teachers. He has probably washed more blackboards than the average janitor.

So Willie and I slipped into Mr. Barrie's room next door to figure out our next move. And it was at this point that I remembered a conversation I had overheard after lunch when some of the teachers were in the fifth grade classroom hunting for the glasses again.

"If they don't turn up before you leave," said Mr. Barrie to Miss Easter, "I'll drive you home and take care of getting your car to you."

"Thanks very much," said Miss Easter in this unthankful tone. "But I'm sure I'll find them before school closes. And if I don't, I'll just ride home with Alice and leave my car here."

But Miss Crockett, who is also Alice, said, "I have to stay and finish several sets of papers after the meeting. I'll be leaving late." For some reason Miss Crockett winked at Mr. Barrie. Miss Easter didn't see her, but I did.

"Perhaps it will be more convenient all around if I just call a taxi anyway," said Miss Easter.

Mr. Barrie laughed for some reason. "After you get your glasses back," he said, "I'll keep it in mind that a state of war——"

At this point just when the conversation was pepping up, Miss Easter looked at us kids who were standing around listening and told us to go to our seats. The bell hadn't even rung yet.

Anyway, remembering this conversation, I decided that since there was a chance that Mr. Barrie was the one stuck with driving Miss Easter home, I would put the glasses on his desk. That way he could find them, and it would save him the trip. After we got outside again, Willie complained because he said that the whole matter had caused even more excitement than he had hoped for, and we were losing the chance of a lifetime. But personally I was glad that it was all over.

Chapter VII
A THIEF IN SCHOOL

So you can imagine how I felt the next morning when there was Miss Easter still bumping into things. Willie and I could hardly believe our own eyes. There was a regular search going on all over the building, with even the janitors helping, because Miss Easter said that at first she had thought she laid the glasses on her desk but now the more she tried to remember, the less she was sure where she had taken them off.

"What's going on anyway?" said Willie when we got

together at recess. "Do you suppose Mr. Barrie found out that Miss Easter hates him and so he is paying her back by keeping her glasses?"

"That's impossible," I said, "because he's probably stuck with driving her home. Somebody took those glasses before he got back to his room."

"Then there is a thief in school," said Willie, looking pleased, "an honest-to-goodness thief."

"And we've got a case," I said. "We're responsible for those glasses."

"I don't feel responsible," said Willie. "We put them back."

"I mean because we're the only detectives in school," I said.

"What I mostly feel responsible for," said Willie, "is Ronald making all that money."

What Willie meant was that Ronald had brought a bunch of comic books to school and was renting them at two cents a magazine. The day before, when Ronald was looking cross-eyed, he had been testing Miss Easter's nearsightedness in case the information would ever come in handy. I mean, most people would look cross-eyed just for fun. But Ronald is the kind of person who always has a purpose. And sure enough, he'd been able to pass the comic books around the room and collect all morning, and Miss Easter hadn't noticed a thing, except to compliment us on how quiet we were. I will admit that they were good comic books—all pretty gory.

Anyway, Willie and I decided to get together later and work on our theories. That is, Willie already had a theory that the jewels on the male Io were real and that a gang of jewel thieves had heard about them. I didn't have any theory yet, but I figured I'd have one by noon. But I thought all day, and the only person I could think of who would have a reason for taking Miss Easter's glasses was Willie, which shows what a tough case this was. After school Willie and I were sitting on the curb in front of my house thinking some more, when Miss Easter and Mr. Barrie drove by with Ronald Pruitt sitting in the back seat of Mr. Barrie's car. Miss Easter and Mr. Barrie waved to us, and Ronald stuck out his tongue, turned his eyes inside out, and wiggled his fingers from the side of his head. We watched as Mr. Barrie drove into Ronald's driveway.

"Look at that," said Willie. "That's what you get when you wash the blackboard. He wouldn't be such a teacher's pet if she knew that he made forty-six cents today renting comic books."

Mr. Barrie turned the car around after letting Ronald get out, and they drove past, waving again and looking very smiley.

"Look at that," said Willie. "I don't get it. Driving to school with him and home again in the afternoon after everything she said. Somebody ought to tell Mr. Barrie how she hates him. Maybe she stole those eyeglasses herself so she could save on gas."

"No," I said. "You've got to admit that even though she doesn't like Homer and Mr. Barrie, she isn't the thieving type. But there are a lot of queer things about this case. I keep having the funny feeling that something is going to happen. To us, I mean. It keeps me from concentrating. I don't like Ronald's look. Did you notice his expression at school today?"

"Yeah," said Willie. "He looked that way at Freddie's birthday party when Homer VII turned up in the bottom of the pitcher of lemonade and I got spanked just because Homer was my frog."

"And the time someone let the air out of Uncle Fred's front tires and left my tool kit by the wheel," I said.

"He had that same look that time at Children's Day Exercises," said Willie, "when you and Betsy Miller were singing a duet and a garter snake somebody had put in your pocket crawled out onto Betsy's bare arm right in the middle of a high note."

Willie and I know Ronald, all right. Whenever he gets a certain look, it means something unpleasant is sure to happen to an innocent bystander—namely Willie and me.

"He would be thinking up something right now when we have to keep our minds on the case," Willie said. "Do you suppose that he is planning to find the glasses himself and muscle us out of the detective business?"

"He doesn't want them found," I said. "His comic book business is too good."

And that's when the explanation for the missing glasses hit me.

"Willie!" I said.

"Don't bust my eardrum," said Willie in a sort of depressed manner, Ronald being a depressing subject.

"When we go swimming," I said, "does Ronald ever go into the water first?"

"Of course not. He waits until someone else sees how cold it is. Everybody knows that."

"At scout camp when Jackie Carr is cook, does Ronald ever take the first bite?"

"You know he doesn't," said Willie. "He never takes a chance. What are you getting at?"

"Well, he brought those comic books to school this morning!" I said. "How did he know that Miss Easter wouldn't find her glasses all of a sudden and catch him in the act?"

This was really peculiar if you knew Ronald the way Willie and I know Ronald. I mean, Ronald is careful. Willie got the point right away, but he didn't get the answer. He stared at me with his mouth open. This was the time we looked the most like two detectives.

"He was cleaning blackboards yesterday afternoon," I said. "So who had a chance to go snooping around during teachers' meeting?"

Willie slapped himself so hard that accidentally, as he discovered later, he killed Homer XVIII. None of Willie's frogs live very long.

"Andy," he said, "you are a natural-born detective. Boy, what a brain! We've got it. Ronald is the thief."

"But now how are we going to prove it?" I said.

"You could wrestle him down tomorrow during recess and go through his pockets. I'll watch for teachers."

"Ronald wouldn't have the goods on him. He wouldn't take a chance like that. What we have to do is get into his mind. He's planning something."

"I'm not getting into a mind like that," said Willie. "Imagine stealing Miss Easter's glasses. How low-down can a person get?"

So we agreed that next day in school I would take the dirty job and concentrate on the inside of Ronald's head while Willie kept an eye on his hands and feet. But twenty-four hours later we had to admit that we were not any closer to figuring out what Ronald had done with the glasses or just what he was plotting. All day he had tended to his comic book business, and when he wasn't making change, he was making a good impression. Ronald is the type who likes to wave his hand in the air and recite. But all the time he had this look I mentioned that he gets when something is going to happen to Willie or me. It would have made anybody but us nervous.

We were talking about this on the way home from school that day when suddenly Willie slapped his pockets. "Jeepers," he said, "I was so busy keeping an eye on Ronald that I forgot and left Homer XIX in my desk. I've got to go back for him. He hates school so far."

As it turned out for us, it was a good thing Willie was absentminded that day. We decided that it would be more interesting to go back through the window. Our classroom was on the ground floor, but when we'd worked our way around the building behind the shrubbery, we found that the windows were too high for Willie to get through one, even with help. But I could make it if Willie got on his hands and knees and I stood on his back.

I climbed up and looked into the room. Miss Easter was there at her desk grading papers, and of course there was Ronald Pruitt washing the blackboard. Everything was quiet except for the sound of the sponge swishing across the board. But it was funny. Ronald, who had his back to me, kept looking over his far shoulder at Miss Easter and washing the same piece of blackboard.

"What's keeping you?" whispered Willie. "My back's breaking."

Just then Miss Easter got up and left the room. The minute the door swung to, Ronald shot over to the brief-case which he had brought the comic books to school in. He got something out of the briefcase, and then he rushed to Willie's desk and lifted the lid. Right at this point Willie's back gave way. However, we didn't make any noise because luckily for us I landed on Willie's head. Willie's worst fault as a detective is wanting to talk all the time. So while I was still on his head, I whispered to him to be quiet because Ronald was in his desk and we had to find out why. It turned out that Willie was too stunned right then to talk anyway.

We waited for Ronald to leave, and in a few minutes we saw him come out of the school building carrying his briefcase. He had this look that always meant bad luck for Willie and me, and he had it so strong that you could almost hear him ticking. We waited until he was out of sight. Then I climbed in through the window.

I had just opened Willie's desk when I heard Miss Easter's voice in the hall. I wanted to run, but I didn't. A detective has to stay cool, even if he's wrapped up in ce-ment and thrown into a river. So although Willie's desk was full of odds and ends and although I wasn't sure what I was looking for and although Miss Easter's voice was getting closer, I kept on investigating. There had to be some reason for Ronald's interest in Willie's desk.

Miss Easter had almost reached the door when down in the corner of the desk under the remains of a cheese sandwich I saw a glasses case. I grabbed it and made it through the window just as Miss Easter opened the class-room door. It was a close shave. Willie took one look at my face as I came through the window and just naturally left in a hurry. We ran until we got to the alley behind my house.

"What are we running for?" said Willie.

"Miss Easter almost caught me," I said. "I found this in your desk."

"In my desk?" said Willie. "I never saw it before. What's in it?"

I opened the case. And there were Miss Easter's glasses.

Chapter VIII

WILLIE AND I FOIL A FRAME-UP

Well, we had found the glasses and discovered the identity of the thief and solved the case, but we went to school the next morning feeling rather depressed. Somehow, we couldn't inform even on Ronald, even though it was a pretty sure thing that he had been making arrangements for an innocent person like Willie to get the blame for what he, Ronald, had done. It looked as if all we could do was to slip the glasses back to Miss Easter and no one would ever know what good detectives we were or the truth about Ronald.

But it all turned out different because of Mr. Barrie's hanging around Miss Easter's desk until after the bell rang. I'd have taken a chance on putting the glasses back if only Miss Easter had been there, but Mr. Barrie's eyes are too good. So class started with me still stuck with the glasses.

In the excitement of the afternoon before, we had forgotten all about Homer XIX. We were reminded of him suddenly when Betsy Miller opened her desk just after Miss Easter took attendance and Homer leaped out. He hit against Betsy's neck, then fell into her lap, then hit her neck again. Homer XIX was a good jumper. But Willie said later that Homer XIX turned out to be the most nervous frog he ever had, and he thought that it was all a result of Betsy Miller's screeching. Willie said that Betsy gave Homer a shock from which he never recovered.

Anyway, the upshot of all this—after Willie got bawled out for ten minutes—was that Miss Easter said we would have desk inspection. Ronald, with this look on his face, went to get the wastebasket. Ronald always carried the wastebasket when we had desk inspection as a reward for having the neatest desk in the room.

Planting Homer on Betsy Miller was really a slick way for Ronald to arrange for desk inspection. You've got to hand it to Ronald. He may be a creep, but he's not a dumb creep. That's why I was in such a tight spot. Teachers always put Willie and me in the front of the room, and so Willie was sitting in the first seat in the first row with me right behind him. Miss Easter always started desk inspection with Willie, and I knew that when the glasses case didn't turn up in Willie's desk, Ronald would be looking around and would be sure to see the big bulge in my jeans pocket.

I didn't know what to do, and I had to do something fast. Ronald's desk was right across from mine in the second row, and so while he was on his way to get the waste-basket, I slipped the glasses case into his desk. Nobody noticed except Freddie Clark because everybody else was busy trying to clean up his desk before inspection except Freddie, who knew he couldn't. But Freddie never tells on anybody. You could twist Freddie's arm off up to the socket, and he wouldn't squeal. What I intended to do after Miss Easter and Ronald had passed me and were at the back of the first row was to get the glasses again.

But it was funny the way it worked out. I didn't have any intention of planting those glasses on Ronald, who was guilty, even though he had planted them on Willie, who was innocent. I mean there are some things you just don't do unless you are a creep. But what happened, Willie was emptying his desk and Ronald was pretending to help him and Miss Easter, who was standing between my desk and Ronald's, was saying, "For goodness' sake, Willie," over a supply of chewed bubble gum. Miss Easter always got so worked up over Willie's desk that I couldn't see why she wanted to look. But anyway all of a sudden, while she was bawling Willie out for the cheese sandwich and a large, dead beetle, she said, "I wish, Willie, that you'd try to follow Ronald's example. Just see how neat and orderly Ronald's desk is."

She lifted the lid of Ronald's desk as she said this. I suppose most of the time Miss Easter wouldn't have paid much attention to a glasses case on top of Ronald's books, but she couldn't quite see what it was. So she picked it up, and then in an absentminded sort of way, I suppose having glasses on her mind, she opened the case. She stared at them.

45

"My glasses!" she said.

It was probably one of the biggest shocks that Ronald Pruitt ever had. His head was down in Willie's desk, and he came out looking as if he had just swallowed a woolly-worm. It was a shock to Miss Easter, too. She put the glasses on, and then for almost a full minute she stood and looked at Ronald like Betsy Miller looking at Homer XIX. Then she gave the rest of us an assignment and led Ronald into a little room where she takes us to improve our character. They were still there when the recess bell rang. Miss Easter came out and dismissed us. She was looking upset. We caught a glimpse of Ronald. He was looking calm. Ronald never sweats. The door wasn't quite shut when Miss Easter went back into the little room, and so Willie and I slipped behind the door and listened.

"Now let me see whether I have this story straight," Miss Easter was saying. "You found the glasses on Mr. Barrie's desk. But later you were afraid to give them to me because you thought I wouldn't believe that you had found them there, since Mr. Barrie hadn't returned them. So after putting them into a case to protect them for me, you didn't know what to do. And the reason you spent so much time when we first came in here denying any knowledge of the glasses was that you didn't think I would believe the truth."

"That's it," said Ronald.

The world isn't safe with people like Ronald Pruitt in it. Willie and I went as fast as we could to find Mr. Barrie. There wasn't anything to do but warn him so that he could be ready to explain to the police. With Ronald framing him and Miss Easter hating him the way she did,

Mr. Barrie was in real trouble. We found him in his room and told him the whole story.

At first, Mr. Barrie had trouble realizing the danger he was in. He had such a bad cold that he kept having to turn away to blow his nose and cough, and I suppose that this kept him from concentrating on the seriousness of the situation. But finally he understood the whole thing. Under stress, Willie remembered a lot more of the conversation he had overheard that day when Homer XVIII got loose, and it certainly showed that Miss Easter was Mr. Barrie's enemy, all about how conceited he was and how he took people for granted.

"She really hates you," said Willie.

"I hadn't realized how much," said Mr. Barrie, blowing his nose. "I hope that you, as reliable private eyes, will regard the matter as confidential."

Of course we said we would.

"And remember," said Willie, "my taking the glasses was Miss Easter's own idea, since she said that men should make things happen, not just wait for them to happen."

"And we put them back because of our fathers' ideas," I said.

"I'll keep all that in mind," said Mr. Barrie. "Your decision to put them back was the right one. In special circumstances Miss Easter's idea might be helpful, but I hope that I can count on your being guided in the future by your fathers' ideas."

Of course we said he could.

"Now if your part in the case is known," said Mr. Barrie, "there might be some people who won't realize how much you are in favor of law and order. So if you can do without the publicity of having solved the case, I think that I can give Miss Easter an explanation about her glasses which will not involve you."

"We'll stand by you," said Willie, "if you need us. We'll be ready to swear in court that Ronald Pruitt was the real thief."

Mr. Barrie was all choked up with this bad cold, but he finally managed to tell us through his handkerchief that he could handle the situation, now that we had given him some information he hadn't had before.

That's about all of our second big case, which we never got any publicity for as Mr. Barrie thought it better to keep it private. I don't know what he told Miss Easter, but Willie thinks that since women teachers have a tendency to like you when you're sick, Mr. Barrie worked on her sympathies with that terrible cold he had. However, the peculiar thing was that he kept driving her to school even after she got her glasses back, and she is now wearing a diamond engagement ring which he gave her. She must have decided to overlook the fact that Mr. Barrie is not the kind of person who makes things happen.

Just the other day I asked Mr. Barrie whether it would be safe and ethical now to tell what happened. He said he thought it was safe and he'd leave the ethics of the case up to anyone who heard about it, with a plea for leniency for all four culprits. He explained these words to me, but I don't get it. Ronald is naturally a culprit, and you might stretch a point and call Willie and me culprits, but why blame Homer XVIII? He was dead most of the time anyway.

Chapter IX
FREDDIE CLARK LOOKS AHEAD

When Mr. Barrie found out that Willie and I were in the detective business, he suggested that we might like to read about the career of Sherlock Holmes. I have been reading Sherlock Holmes's cases ever since, and they are really neat. Of course, Sherlock Holmes had a lot of breaks that Willie and I haven't had. For one thing, he lived where all the people are foreigners, and Mr. McCotter says that foreigners are always needing help. Practically every day somebody drove up to Sherlock Holmes's door in a dogcart asking for help. People just don't do things like that in Wakanda. I asked Mr. McCotter why people around here don't do interesting things like keeping poisonous snakes in safes, and he said that the reason is that most of the people around here are Republicans. Mr. McCotter says that Willie and I would get more business if there were more Democrats around. But even though Willie and I haven't had the breaks, Sherlock Holmes would have to admit that several of Willie's and my cases have been singular, especially the third big case.

About a week after Willie and I solved the mystery of Miss Easter's missing eyeglasses, we were sitting in our detective agency office in my father's garage counting the money in the treasury and staying away from Willie's mother, who was down on Willie because she was mad at

49

his father. Willie said the mood his mother was in, just about the time we got a big murder case to solve, she would think of twenty-five other things for him to do. All the money we had was eighteen cents left from a case we had solved the day before when Aunt Gertrude had asked us to find her cat, Blossom. Blossom is so touchy that I personally doubted that she wanted to be found, but if you're a detective, you don't refuse to find a missing person just because you or he is glad he is. As it turned out, Morris Somers, who is very scientific, had made a new rocket and was all ready to send Blossom into orbit. He was just starting on the countdown, he told us, when his mother sent him to the grocery. And while he was gone, Jackie Carr's little sister, who wanted to be the first in the neighborhood to go into orbit, stole the rocket containing Blossom. Morris said that if it hadn't been for Jackie's little sister, Blossom would have been in outer space in no time.

As it was, we found the rocket in Jackie Carr's bushes. Blossom was looking in a disapproving way through a window Morris had made for her so she could admire the stars, and so we delivered her to Aunt Gertrude nailed up. I mean, someone with a disposition like Blossom's you don't set free for nothing. But after Aunt Gertrude had paid us a quarter for finding Blossom, she offered another for unnailing her. Blossom managed to scratch us both on the way out. If Morris had launched Blossom, she would have been the maddest cat in orbit. Blossom isn't the type that wants to be a star.

Anyway, on this Friday afternoon after school, Willie and I were sitting in our office wishing we could get a case like the one on *Big City Detective* on television the night before, where a rich millionaire gave the detective a thousand-dollar retainer to investigate his sister. So it was quite a coincidence when Freddie Clark, who gets the biggest allowance in our neighborhood, came to hire us to investigate his sister. First, Freddie gave us a dollar retainer. You can always count on Freddie to just naturally know how things are done. Besides, he never misses *Big City Detective*.

"What's the matter with your sister?" I said.

"That's what I want you to find out," said Freddie. "I want you to detect what's wrong with her. It's a mystery, my mother says."

Then Freddie told us about this conversation he'd overheard between his mother and his father. Freddie says that his mother often comes home from an afternoon at her bridge club with her whole outlook on life ruined by Mrs. Peck, one of her dearest friends. Mrs. Peck's daughter, Mary Annabelle, and Freddie's sister, Susan, are both thirteen and freshmen in high school. And Mrs. Peck had asked who was escorting Susan to the freshman class party, and Freddie's mother, who hadn't heard there was going to be a party, had said what she'd said the year before when Mary Annabelle was escorted to two dancing parties and the summer before when Mary Annabelle was escorted to a swimming party and the month before when Mary Annabelle was escorted to a school mixer after a football game— which was that she thought Susan was still too young to be having dates. Mrs. Peck said that she agreed and that it was certainly wearing to have a popular daughter, but things could be worse, couldn't they.

Freddie's father, who was trying to listen to the television news from the Far East, didn't react much at first to the news from the bridge club, except to say that Freddie's mother had made the right decision about Susan. But then Freddie's mother said but why wasn't Susan being escorted to the class party and why didn't Susan ever tell them about these things. She had just said that Susan was prettier than Mary Annabelle Peck and it was a mystery to her, when suddenly Freddie's father said the world was full of idiots at home and abroad and went to play "Swing Low, Sweet Chariot" on the piano, which meant things were too much for him. Once after an election, Freddie's father played "Swing Low, Sweet Chariot" every night for two weeks. Freddie's father is a nervous person. Anyway, Freddie said that since his mother called it a mystery, he'd decided to put Willie and me on the case.

"Why do you care anyway, Freddie?" said Willie.

"Look at all the advantages Jackie Carr has because his big sister is popular," said Freddie.

I'd never thought about it, but this is true. Jackie Carr is always eating more hot fudge sundaes than are possible on his allowance and always waving from motor scooters and convertibles. Once when his sister, who is in college, had a friend with an airplane, Jackie got to fly over town and buzz the ball park.

"I figure that a popular sister is a good investment," said Freddie. "I intend to find out early what's wrong with her and then improve her."

You've got to hand it to Freddie Clark. He always looks ahead. I suppose Freddie is about the most prepared person I know. Once when we were in a play in the fourth grade, Freddie got the most interesting part of the savage because he was the only one in class who had a necklace of human teeth handy to wear. Freddie had bought everybody's teeth in the neighborhood as they came out. He always looks ahead.

Chapter X
LOOKING FOR A MISSING QUALITY

After Freddie left, Willie said, "How are we going to start finding out what is wrong with a girl? I mean, how do you find a missing quality? It's not like finding a missing body or a missing diamond bracelet or a missing bank president."

"Who's the most popular girl we know?" I said after thinking for a while.

"Barbie Reagan," said Willie.

This was true. Everybody in the fifth grade would have said so.

"What we'll do," I said, "is make a list of the qualities that make Barbie popular and then test Susan for them."

Willie said that this made good sense, and so we made a long list of Barbie's important qualities like her being able to chin herself twenty-four times straight. But then Willie pointed out that it would take too long to test Susan for all of Barbie's qualities. Barbie Reagan could do anything. You hardly ever thought about her being a girl.

So we decided that the most efficient method was to pick out Barbie's two most important qualities to test

Susan for. And we finally decided that if a girl wanted to be popular, she had to be fast and be a good wrestler. These qualities explained just about everything Barbie could do. And as Willie said, they always seem to show up in popular people. For example, my mother is popular with my father and Willie's mother is popular with his father, and if you'd ever been around Willie or me when we did something wrong, you'd have to admit that our mothers are fast and potentially good wrestlers.

Our first test fell through. What happened, we went to Freddie's to play badminton. Freddie has everything in the sports equipment line that you can think of. He is so prepared that he even got his father to put up lights for playing badminton and croquet at night. Practically nobody except Willie and me knew that Freddie had all that equipment because he was always too busy collecting, and Susan was always too busy reading to use it. But we told Freddie that it was important to the case that we see Susan play badminton. You can always count on Freddie Clark. He didn't ask any questions. He saw that we were on the job, and that's what he was paying us for. It took a lot of effort, but Freddie finally got Susan to play.

Well, right away Willie spoiled everything. Freddie and I were playing Willie and Susan, and I was supposed to watch Susan's footwork to detect how fast she was, and Willie was supposed to accidentally hit her with his racket and run into her by accident because good wrestlers have to be able to take a lot of punishment. But Susan started praising Willie's playing, and Willie forgot that he was a detective and became nothing but a badminton player. He is always a tricky player, I'll say that for him,

54

but this time he was all over the court. Every time I hit one to Susan to test her speed, Willie got it. He kept saying, "How was that one, Susan?" And he forgot all about hitting her or knocking her down. It was disgusting.

Then I got another idea. I said I didn't want to play any more, and I asked Susan whether she could do push-ups. But immediately Willie said, "I can. Look at me, Susan," and he started doing push-ups as if he was trying for a gold medal. I don't know what got into Willie. He said later that he didn't know either. Anyway, Susan was praising Willie and counting his push-ups, and when he got up to thirty-four and looked as if he was on the verge of a stroke, I saw that he wasn't going to be in shape to detect and that we might as well leave for the time being. So stepping on his back, I said we had to go.

While we were sitting on my front steps waiting for Willie to get over feeling sick so that we could go back to detecting what was wrong with Susan, Hubert Welsh, who is one of our best friends, came into sight at the far end of the street looking through his binoculars. Hubert publishes a paper called the *News of the World*, and you always know when a new edition is coming out because there is Hubert out looking. When he got directly opposite my house on the other side of the street, he caught sight of Willie and me and stopped and adjusted his lens and looked for a while. I made my man-from-Mars face, but Willie just looked back, which shows the condition he was in.

"You got measles or something, Willie?" said Hubert after a little bit.

"He's been doing push-ups for Susan Clark," I said.

"Thirty-four," said Willie in a sort of croak.

Hubert went away looking disappointed. He always counts a good deal on people's having measles or mumps for the *News of the World.*

Willie never did get to feeling like helping to figure out another test for Susan that day, and so I had to work on a new angle by myself. What I did was to get Freddie to invite me to stay all night at his house. Freddie had sent away for an enormous, hairy, black spider. It looked real but wasn't. Nobody had seen it but Willie and me because Freddie intended to try it out on people.

So early the next morning Freddie and I went into Susan's room and put it on her pillow next to her nose. Then we got behind some furniture and made a buzzing noise so she would wake up. I never saw a test work better. Susan opened her eyes right on the spider. Then she looked cross-eyed at it. Then her face sort of went to pieces, and she jumped out of bed backwards, and the next thing we knew she was out of the room and running down the hall to her mother's and father's room. I never saw anybody move so fast. Even Barbie Reagan couldn't have beat her. When Susan got her mother there to see the spider, they took Susan's whole bed apart, but they didn't find anything because Freddie and I had picked up the spider when we left.

Right after breakfast, I was lucky enough to detect quite by accident that Susan also had all the signs of being a good wrestler. Freddie and I had been discussing at breakfast whether a tarantula had teeth or fangs, and after breakfast Blossom walked by, and we decided to count her teeth, since we were on the subject. Blossom, as usual, wouldn't cooperate, and when Susan, who had been jumpy all through breakfast, heard Blossom yelling, she got the idea that Blossom was being tortured. So she came rushing out of the house and threw Freddie clear off the ground in one direction and me in the other. It nearly scared Blossom out of her wits.

Well, I complimented Freddie on Susan's speed and muscle, thanked him for having a good time, thanked his mother, who was in Susan's room pushing furniture around, and told Freddie that the investigation was moving along. Then I went to tell Willie what I had detected.

Chapter XI
A TRICKY PLAN

Willie was looking cheerful that morning, even after I told him that we were going to have to start all over on what was wrong with Susan. He said his mother had apparently decided to let bygones be bygones because she was acting as if she liked him and his father again. What makes his mother so popular around his house, Willie said, is that when she isn't mad, she is so friendly.

It shows how a detective has to think of every little detail. We hadn't remembered that Barbie Reagan is always friendly until Willie made this remark about his mother.

"Since Susan has turned out to be strong and fast,

maybe it's friendliness we should test her for," I said. "Maybe we should make a new list of Barbie's qualities and this time remember everything."

"Why don't we ask the freshman boys what qualities they like in a girl and save our brains?" said Willie.

Willie has really good ideas when it comes to saving his brain. The only problem was what reason we'd give for asking. Detectives have to protect their clients, and it would be embarrassing to Freddie if we explained that one of his relatives had to be investigated. But just then Hubert came along looking through his binoculars, and we had another good idea. We arranged with Hubert to do a column on what freshman boys like about freshman girls in exchange for an advertisement about Willie and me opening a detective agency. Hubert was all for it right away. The motto of the *News of the World* is "We believe in public service."

So Willie and I went around asking questions and explaining that we were writing a column for Hubert Welsh. Some of the freshman boys laughed and wouldn't cooperate, but Willie and I stayed with it, and finally we had a list of about nine qualities, which we figured was plenty. We put down only what we knew was true. I mean, for example, we left out Perry Swanson's dumb idea of a necessary quality, which was *Be a good dancer*. The kind of person Perry Swanson is, he kept looking at himself in the mirror over the soda fountain at Antonelli's all the time he was talking to us, and Willie said if Perry liked what he saw that well, he wouldn't know a good quality if it hit him in the face.

I wish we could have told Sherlock Holmes about

the next detecting situation we planned, for it was really tricky. First, we had to call Freddie in for consultation, since the idea we had was the kind that wouldn't be ethical without Freddie's OK.

"What we want to do," I told Freddie, "is to save time and check on Susan for a whole bunch of qualities at once, and the best way to do it is to fix it so that we can see the way she acts with a whole bunch of boys."

"OK," said Freddie. "How?"

"Sam Holling works for your father as office boy in the summer time, doesn't he, and caddies for him and does odd jobs for him?" I said.

Freddie said that was true.

"And Sam Holling knows everybody and is popular with everybody?" I said.

Freddie said that was true. Sam is the best tackle on the freshman football team. And Freddie's father had once said to Freddie's mother that you could always count on Sam to have a heart of solid gold and a head of solid bone. Everybody admires him.

"All right," I said, "I call Sam on the telephone this afternoon, and I say I'm you."

"That's not true," said Freddie.

"You hired me, didn't you?" I said, which Freddie had to admit was true. "I represent you, don't I?" I said, which Freddie had to admit was true. "All right, then what does 'represent' mean? Look it up in the dictionary."

"He's got you, Freddie," said Willie.

Freddie had to admit that considering what 'represent' means, it was ethical for me to say that I was Freddie.

"Of course," I said, "you must plan to spend all afternoon with somebody who will give you an alibi for the phone call."

"Why?" said Freddie.

"Wait," I said. "Now I tell Sam Holling that my father—that's your father—would like to give a surprise party for Susan tonight."

"That isn't true," said Freddie.

"We're not saying you're going to give it. We're saying you'd like to give it," said Willie. "Anyone would like to surprise somebody."

Freddie said that was true.

"So I say that my mother—that's your mother—is out of town and can't call people to arrange for a party," I said.

Freddie said this was true. His mother and Aunt Gertrude were leaving that afternoon for a garden club convention and wouldn't be back until the next day. I'd heard about it because I had to go to Aunt Gertrude's to feed Blossom.

"And my father—that's your father—is not going to be home until dinner time and is too busy to call people."

Freddie said this was true.

"So I say that we want him—that's Sam Holling—to call the boys on the list we give him."

"Who's we?" said Freddie.

"You and Willie and I," I said. "But I won't emphasize that."

"Oh," said Freddie. "OK, that's true."

"Then I tell Sam that we want him to get as many of them as possible to come to Susan's house to surprise her and to see that it is kept quiet because we don't want Susan to hear about it. Then I give him a list of about twenty-five boys so that even at the last minute like this we can be sure of some of them coming. And then Willie and I can be on hand to detect what makes Susan unpopular so you can correct it."

Freddie said that since there wasn't any lying or dishonesty involved, it was all right with him.

"The queer thing is," said Willie, "that even though it's all true, I've got a feeling it might get us into trouble. I've got a feeling that my mother would kill me."

You can't ever ignore Willie's hunches. We all sat and thought it over. Finally I said if we were going to be detectives we had to be brave enough to take chances as long as everything was ethical, especially since we were doing good. But Freddie said that he wasn't a detective.

"What could happen?" he said. "What happens when they get to my house? Let's look ahead."

"OK," I said. "Pretend you're Susan. Pretend I'm coming to your house to a party you never heard of. So I ring the doorbell. You come to the door. I would say, 'Surprise. I've come to the party.' What would you say?"

" 'Who's giving a party?' " said Freddie.

"So I'd say, 'Your father.' Then what would you do?"

"I'd ask my father, and he'd say he wasn't giving a party, so I'd say to you, 'Nobody here is giving a party.' "

"So I'd say, 'Freddie said this afternoon on the phone that there was going to be a party here.' "

"Then I'd say, 'Freddie was with me all afternoon. Someone has got things mixed up,' " said Freddie.

61

"So I'd say, 'OK,' and leave."

There didn't seem to be a loophole in it. And all through this conversation Willie and I would be having a chance to watch Susan in a social situation. Freddie said it seemed to him that the plan was both safe and ethical and went home to arrange an alibi.

Willie and I called Sam Holling right after lunch when we went to Aunt Gertrude's to feed Blossom. Sam said that he was glad to help Mr. Clark out and he'd do his best.

Chapter XII
A SURPRISE PARTY

That night Willie and I went to Freddie's house after dinner. We were playing dominoes down in the recreation room when the doorbell rang. Earlier, Freddie had been working on his father for a tennis court since the government statistics said that we're all out of condition. But his father said that he couldn't see the advantage of being in condition when the bomb hit us. Freddie's father worries a lot about the bomb. So for the time being, Freddie had dropped the subject of the tennis court so that his father would get his mind off the bomb that was about to hit him, and when the doorbell rang, we were playing dominoes and Freddie's father was reading and Susan was watching a television play about a man and a woman in the far North, which from where I sat looked pretty mushy. When the bell rang, nobody moved. Freddie and Willie and I looked at one another. The doorbell rang again.

"Is that the doorbell?" said Willie, which it certainly was.

"See who's there," said Freddie's father, not looking up from his book.

Susan didn't budge.

"Freddie," said his father.

"Who, me?" said Freddie.

The doorbell rang again. Mr. Clark looked at Freddie.

"Why can't Susan answer it?" said Freddie. "She's not doing anything."

The doorbell rang again.

"Freddie," said Mr. Clark in this voice.

"I'll answer it," said Freddie as if there hadn't been any discussion.

"Me, too," said Willie.

So we all three went to the door. It was Perry Swanson all dressed up as if he were going somewhere.

"Am I the first one here?" whispered Perry.

"Just a minute," said Freddie.

We went back to the recreation room.

"It's for you," Freddie told Susan. "It's Perry Swanson."

"What does he want?" said Susan, not taking her eyes off the screen where the man and the woman were hugging in a snowstorm.

The doorbell rang again.

"Well, for heaven's sake, find out," said Mr. Clark, "so we can have some quiet."

Susan got up slowly, still watching the screen where the man and the woman were saying good-bye. "I would have to miss the best part," said Susan.

We all three followed Susan to the door. Sam Holling and two other boys were there with Perry. Susan looked as surprised as if it were a surprise party.

"Hello," she said, opening the door.

"Hello," the boys said, coming in.

Susan looked at the boys. The boys looked around the room. Sam Holling winked at Freddie and raised his eyebrows, but Freddie pretended he didn't see him. The doorbell rang, and through the windows we could see several boys at the door.

"Won't you sit down?" said Susan, looking even more surprised and going back to the door.

"Where's your dad?" whispered Sam to Freddie, but Freddie pretended he didn't hear him.

We hadn't figured on everybody being dressed up and getting inside the house. It was like a detective case all right, like when the detective gets all the culprits together in one room and then solves the case, except that I had the feeling that the detective wasn't there yet. Just as Susan got back with four more boys, the doorbell rang again.

"I think I'll go home," Willie said to me. "It's getting too crowded in here." But he couldn't get out right then because there were so many people coming in.

"Where's your father?" said Sam to Susan. "Will you let him know we're here?"

We all three followed Susan back to the recreation room.

"I think I'll go to bed," Freddie whispered to me.

"Don't worry," I told him. "Willie and I always protect our clients."

"I can't stay too long," said Willie.

64

As we went into the room, the doorbell rang.

"What's the matter with that boy?" said Freddie's father.

"It's for you," said Susan.

"Who, me?" said Freddie's father. "Perry Swanson?"

The doorbell rang again.

"Great Scot," said Freddie's father. "What's his trouble? Is he caught in the doorbell?"

"It's a lot of boys," said Susan. "They keep coming. Sam Holling said to tell you they were here."

Freddie's father went upstairs. Freddie and Willie and I followed him. There must have been about sixteen boys in the room by that time. They all stood up and grinned and nodded at Freddie's father, who looked as if a tiger had just said hello to him. Susan was answering the door, and Sam Holling said in a whisper to Freddie's father, "I got in touch with all of them, Mr. Clark. Most of them are here."

"Oh yes," said Freddie's father, "I see they are."

"Four guys that were on the list you gave Freddie to phone me this afternoon couldn't come," said Sam. "But I got hold of all the rest. I told them if you gave a party, it would really be a party. Shall we yell surprise at Susan now or wait for the others?"

"Just a minute," said Freddie's father, taking Freddie by the shoulder. "We have to have a conference," he explained to Sam, shoving Freddie ahead of him out of the room.

Willie and I followed Freddie and his father. We weren't afraid that Freddie would get us into trouble because Freddie Clark is the type you could pull his thumbnails out and he wouldn't squeal on anybody. But we thought his father would be less likely to kill him if there were witnesses. Mr. Clark was looking plenty tough.

"What did you tell Sam on the telephone this afternoon?" said Freddie's father.

"I didn't tell him anything," said Freddie. "I didn't call him on the telephone. I wasn't even here this afternoon. Susan and I went to a movie. Ask her," he said, because just then Susan appeared looking pink.

"There are nineteen boys here, Daddy," she said, "and I think they've come to give me a surprise party. Isn't it exciting? What should I do?"

The doorbell rang. Freddie's father put his hands over his ears. "Answer the bell," he said.

When Susan was gone, he said, "Sam wouldn't make up a story like that. Somebody has played a trick on him and all those boys and Susan. I'd like to get my hands on the joker."

Willie and Freddie and I looked at our shoes. Willie said later he could feel his heart beating in all sorts of queer places.

"Why can't Susan just tell them it's a mistake and there isn't any party?" I said.

"No, no," said Freddie's father. "To say nothing of several other reasons against it, how would you feel if you got all ready for a party and then were told to go home because it was all a mistake?"

We hadn't thought of it from that angle. How were we to know that all of those dumb guys would get so ready?

"So, Freddie," said his father, "you don't know anything about this business."

Freddie didn't say anything. His father looked at him. "Do you?"

"I didn't phone him," said Freddie. "I was at a movie."

"Do you know anything about what happened?"

"Sure," said Freddie. "The cattlemen were having a feud with——"

"Here," said Mr. Clark, getting a look in his eyes.

Freddie didn't say anything. His father shook him. Freddie didn't say a word. That's the way Freddie is. You could run a bulldozer over him, and he wouldn't say anything before or after.

"Answer me," said Mr. Clark.

Freddie didn't say anything. His father gave him such a whack on the underside that the money in Freddie's pockets jingled.

"Answer me," said Mr. Clark.

Freddie didn't say anything. His father picked him up by the collar. I couldn't stand it any longer. Freddie was my client, and besides he was innocent.

"I did it," I said.

"Me, too," said Willie.

"I hired them," said Freddie. "They were representing me."

The doorbell rang.

Freddie's father looked at us, still holding Freddie by the collar. It was one of the most dangerous moments in Willie's and my detective career.

67

"They were supposed just to come to the door and say, 'Surprise,' and then Susan would say something which would help us to detect her missing quality, and then they would go away. They didn't do what they were supposed to do," I said.

"It wasn't a trick," said Willie. "It was a test."

"Start again," said Freddie's father. "Try to make sense."

So we told him about Willie and me being detectives and about Freddie hiring us to find out what was wrong with Susan because his mother said it was a mystery and how in an ethical way we got the boys to come to Freddie's so that we could study Susan's qualities and find out what was missing and help her to be popular.

Freddie's father looked at the ceiling as if somebody there had news for him. "Oh Lord," he said.

The doorbell rang. Mr. Clark groaned. "Can I count on you not to tell Susan or anybody else about this?" he said after a while.

We told him that he could always count on us.

"All right," said Freddie's father. "I'll have a talk with you later. Right now, we'll give a party."

Chapter XIII
HUBERT GETS OUT A SPECIAL EDITION

It was the best party I ever went to. Except for Susan, it was a party for men, and everybody got to do what he wanted to do because there was nobody around organiz-

68

ing you. Tubby Larson, who slept all evening in one corner of the recreation room and didn't wake up until it was time to eat, said himself that it was the best party he ever went to, and he's had a lot of experience because he goes wherever there are refreshments. Even Richard Addams, who read all evening, said that it was the only kind of party that made sense. While Freddie was showing everybody where his sports equipment was and Willie was tuning in on *Mystery of the Week* for mystery lovers and Susan was helping Perry Swanson find records he liked and I was keeping an eye on Susan's social qualities, Freddie's father called Mr. Antonelli, who came and brought a gallon of ice cream and crates of soft drinks and other things and helped Freddie's father get going. Mr. Clark got his outdoor grill in order and sent Sam Holling for meat and buns and whatever else Sam thought the boys would like. And Sam came back with about a ton of hamburger and other things, including ten watermelons. Willie and I got to stay for the whole party since when our mothers called and we hadn't eaten yet, Freddie got them to let us stay at his house all night because his father needed our help.

The next day was Sunday. About six-thirty in the morning Willie and Freddie and I went into Freddie's father's room to see whether he wanted to have that talk with us before Willie and I went home. He didn't. So we told him that whenever he got around to wanting to have the talk with us, we would be right across the street. And we thanked him for inviting us to his party and told him that Freddie was going to my house for breakfast. He couldn't seem to get into focus. It's a funny thing how grown-ups hate to wake up, though sleeping isn't any fun. But he may have been tired. He must have cooked two hundred hamburgers because I ate six myself. Freddie's father is a terrific cook, as everybody knows now.

After Sunday School, Willie and I checked over our list on Susan, hoping before we reported the bad news to Freddie, to find out that we had made a mistake. While we were checking, Freddie came to tell us that his mother was home again finding damage. That's the kind of person Freddie's mother is. Freddie said she kept talking especially about marks on a table, which was where Freddie was keeping his empty coke bottles when we were having the contest to see who could drink the most; and a cracked lamp, which was the one accidentally knocked over when I tripped on a light cord sneaking behind a chair to eavesdrop on Susan's conversation; and some mustard stains on a chair, which was where Willie sat when he was watching The *Spider Man from Venus* on the late show. Freddie said that his father was going to have a bad time of it when he came home from his golf game, because his mother said that Freddie's father must be losing his mind.

We hated to tell Freddie the truth about Susan, considering what a job of correction it would mean for him, especially when his mother was being a problem and his father was maybe losing his mind. But there was no help for it. So we could give Freddie a businesslike report, we had made a list of the qualities the freshman boys had mentioned, and opposite each quality we had written the answer in relation to Susan and mentioned an example to prove it. The answer was wrong every single time, as

70

this following copy of the report we gave to Freddie will show.

1. *Not be dumb. Not be silly.* Is. Danced the frug with Perry Swanson when she had a chance to play croquet with Willie. 2. *Not be conceited.* Is. Told me to stop spying on her all the time. 3. *Be friendly.* Isn't. Didn't offer to take Willie's part when the big guys wouldn't let him play table tennis. 4. *Not be two-faced.* Is. Didn't offer to take Willie's part, though she knows what a good player he is, when the big guys wouldn't let him play badminton. 5. *Not be stuck-up.* Is. Was very stuck-up toward Willie when he complained because the big guys wouldn't let him play cards with them. 6. *Be good-looking. Be neat.* Isn't. Got to looking very cross at Willie and me all the time. Also was wearing dungarees with a hole in the right knee at a big party. 7. *Not be bossy.* Is. Told Freddie for heaven's sake to do something about Willie and me.

There is no getting around the facts. It was obvious why Susan wasn't popular. She wasn't popular even with Willie and me. But when we told Freddie the truth, he faced up to the facts in the right way as you'd expect Freddie to. He paid us the rest of what we charge for a case and told us that he was a satisfied customer. He said that it wasn't our fault that Susan was a complete loss.

Just as he made this last remark, Hubert Welsh came into sight looking through his binoculars, and the two things happening together gave me an idea which was

71

probably the best deduction Willie and I made during the whole case. Detectives do good, and what had bothered me about the way the investigation of Susan had turned out was that though by the time Freddie got Susan corrected, we would have done good in the long run, our detecting was resulting in a hard job for Freddie in the future. I mean, the good wasn't obvious the way it is in a happy ending, as in the case where Sherlock Holmes whips the poisonous snake so that it goes back up the bell rope and murders the murderer.

What I realized suddenly was that Susan wasn't a complete loss and that probably nobody knew this but Willie and me. What was wrong with her had turned out to be easy to detect. Where we had had the most trouble was detecting her popular qualities. In short, anybody could see that she was two-faced and bossy, but how many people had detected that she was fast and a good wrestler? So I deducted that most people didn't know about these popular qualities, and I deducted that if they did, Susan would be more popular, and Freddie wouldn't have to work so hard. I also deducted that since Hubert's *News of the World* had a pretty wide circulation, and since detectives should have a constructive approach, we could give Susan a break almost immediately. Willie said later that it was the most complicated deducting that he had ever heard of. He said it was a wonder my head didn't fly apart.

"I just had a news flash from Jackie's little sister that Susan gave a party for one hundred and seventy-four boys," said Hubert to Freddie. "Could I have the guest list for my newspaper?"

"There were only twenty-one," said Freddie. "Andy has the list."

And after I'd given Hubert the names, I said, "Do you have room for a poll?"

"I always have room for a poll," said Hubert. "Polls are a public service."

I wish that Sherlock Holmes could have seen that special edition that Hubert put out. Sherlock Holmes would have detected what nobody else guessed, that two good detective brains were behind that survey and that poll. The success of what we did surprised even Willie and me. Freddie paid us a bonus the next day and said that nobody but us would ever do his detecting because that day at school seven boys asked to escort Susan to the class party, and two more called after school.

What we did was this. The day before when Willie and I had made a survey for Hubert of the qualities that freshman boys like in freshman girls, we had added *Be fast* and *Be a good wrestler* to the list, since nobody had happened to remember them. And we asked Hubert to place the news item on the results of the poll right below the news item on the results of the survey. That way the freshman boys would read first what they thought were the important qualities, and then they would read the news item on the poll. Hubert said OK and what was the news item on the poll, and after we'd taken the poll, I dictated it to him: "According to the latest poll conducted in this city, Susan Clark is one of the fastest girls and one of the best wrestlers anywhere around." We would have been able to put down the fastest and the best, but Hubert held out for Barbie Reagan.

Well, Hubert said that he never put out an edition that was more in demand. He said that it had always been his dream to put out an edition that had appeal for every group in society, and this edition did. For the nature lovers, who in this case turned out to be the little kids and the mothers, the item about Mrs. Clark having a tarantula loose in her house raised a lot of interest. And for the society lovers, who in this case turned out to be the freshman girls, there was great interest in the list of boys attending Mr. Clark's party. And for the lovers of menus and statistics, who turned out to be all the high school boys, there was great interest in what was eaten at Mr. Clark's party, which Freddie told Hubert in detail and which was unusual in print. And for the lovers of news of the business world, there was the item about Mr. Clark, prominent business man of this city, giving a party for twenty-one boys to surprise his daughter. And for the lovers of news of sickness, there was the item about Mrs. Clark going to bed with a headache. And Hubert said, for the sports lovers there was the poll, and for the intelligentsia there was the survey. I don't know about the survey appealing to the intelligentsia, who are some people Hubert's father considers un-American, but it and the poll certainly appealed to the freshman boys, as Susan Clark's present-day popularity proves. Because what else could explain it?

So that's the story of Willie's and my third big case and how we detected what was wrong with Freddie's sister and what was good about her and then deducted her into popularity. Hubert's mother, who doesn't seem to have much news sense generally, made him get out another edition and report who took the survey and who added the last two qualities to it and who participated in the poll and who the runner-up in the poll was. But Hubert didn't mind because he said that his newspaper had started selling like hot cakes. Besides, by the time of the next edition, there was more news—like Susan Clark having sixteen invitations to the class party, and Mr. Peck giving a party to surprise his daughter Mary Annabelle, and Freddie's father taking Freddie and Willie and Hubert and me to a big football game. Also, there was an important news story for lovers of science and patriots interested in the new frontier because Morris Somers was announcing to the public that he was starting work on a big missile and was planning to launch Jackie Carr's little sister into outer space as soon as possible.

Willie said he wished that we could do something to get some public acclaim like Morris, but I pointed out that somebody had to straighten out the problems and clear up the mysteries of the world, and that's what we did, even if it wasn't anything flashy like launching someone into orbit. And Willie had to admit it was true.

Chapter XIV
RONALD WINS A PRIZE

The biggest headache Willie and I had when we went into the detective business was our parents. Usually they didn't know much about our detecting because our early cases were all rather private. But every time they got wind of something constructive we'd done in the detective line, they kicked up a fuss. For example, it somehow leaked through to our parents that Willie and I were connected with Hubert's newspaper article on Freddie's sister. You'd think that they'd be pleased to know that we'd succeeded in making Susan popular, but they acted as if Willie and I had dropped a hydrogen bomb or thrown a baseball through Aunt Gertrude's window. It just shows you can't please everybody.

Our parents are dead set against our getting successful and famous. But if you want to be great, you can't let anything discourage you. And as Willie says, some day when we are the greatest detectives in the world, maybe our fathers will apologize for making things so tough for us. But in the meantime, their attitude has created a problem. They said that they didn't want to hear any more about our being in the detective business, and it has certainly cramped our style to have to keep them from hearing about it.

What I'm driving at is why Willie and I didn't completely solve our fourth big case. Ronald Pruitt is always trying to run Willie and me down as detectives. But actually the only mystery that ever completely stumped us was our fourth big case. And it wasn't our fault. What with our fathers being so mad at us for conducting a poll about Susan Clark, we couldn't investigate the mystery of the Halloween thief properly, and what with William Henry Winningham being on our hands, we were under a constant mental strain on the night of the robbery when we would otherwise have been on the alert. Even at that, we made good deductions and got the loot back and returned it to its owners, although nobody ever knew what a good detective job we did except the Geronimoes and all the kids in the neighborhood.

But I must say that although Willie and I have had some funny cases since we went into the detective business, our fourth big case was the funniest we ever had. It was the kind of thing that you can hardly believe even when you know it's true. Sometimes I think that maybe there really is an invisible man like that man on television and that he was in Wakanda last Halloween. It would have to be something unusual like that to explain why Willie and I didn't catch him. That and our fathers and William Henry Winningham.

To start at the beginning, Willie and I always spend a lot of time figuring out how to dress up on Halloween so that we can either scare people to death or tickle them to death. And on this particular Halloween we were especially interested in our costumes because Mr. Bolger was having a party for the kids in the neighborhood early in the evening before we started trick-or-treating and was giving a prize for the best disguise. He said that it would be a short party, just long enough for him to see everybody at once so that he wouldn't have to be opening the door all evening. And Ronald Pruitt had told at school that he had a keen disguise and was going to show Willie and me up. So we really worked on what we were going to wear.

I decided to be a pirate. My disguise was so complicated that it took a lot of preparation. I made a cutlass out of beaver board and painted it silver, and I wore a wide, red silk scarf around my waist to hold up my cutlass.

77

In a trunk in the attic I found a wig which my brother Pete had worn in a play about the American Revolution. At first, I wasn't going to wear it for fear it was sissy, but Willie said it made me look repulsive. So I wore it. I wore short, ragged pants and a striped sweater and boots. But the best part was the scar. I drew this line down my face across my lip which I fixed to curl upside down with Scotch tape. Then I put brown stuff all over my face to hide the tape, and I drew fish and daggers and ships on my arms for tattoo marks and put this brown stuff all over me. If Willie and I hadn't had bad luck, it's a cinch I would have won the prize. I looked revolting.

Willie's disguise was good, too. He wore a big, baggy clown suit with great big flopping shoes. The best thing was that he had a nose with a little wire running to a battery in his pocket. Every time he pressed a button his nose lit up. The first time I saw it I almost died it was so funny.

But as it turned out, we might as well have just put on false faces. First, it took me a lot longer to get ready that night than I had thought it would. My lip wouldn't curl right, and the tattooing and the brown stuff took longer than they had in practice. However, I finally looked horrible. Even my father approved. He was drinking a cup of coffee when I came down the stairs, and when he saw me, he swallowed the wrong way and almost choked to death. He said that I was one of the worst sights he'd ever seen. But it took me a long time to get that way.

Then when I got to Willie's house, Willie wasn't ready. It wasn't Willie's fault. It turned out that William Henry Winningham's mother had called to ask whether William Henry could go with Willie and me. And of all the dumb things to say, Willie's mother had said that we'd be glad to take William Henry along. I don't know where she got the idea. Willie had done his best to explain that a little kid like William Henry would ruin our whole evening, and he was still trying to make his mother see reason when I got there.

"It's not fair," said Willie. "Andy and I won't have any fun at all if we have to drag William Henry around with us."

"Don't exaggerate," said Willie's mother. "If you can't be agreeable enough to take William Henry with you, Willie, you'll just have to stay at home. And if I hear that you haven't been nice to him, I'll take you in hand later."

You can see the kind of thing Willie and I are up against all the time.

Anyway, finally Willie got his disguise on, though he spent so much time complaining that it took quite a while.

"Andy isn't complaining," said Willie's mother. "Why can't you be nice about the prospect of taking William Henry with you the way Andy is?"

What she didn't know was that I was afraid that my scar would come undone if I talked. When we left, Willie was feeling low. He lit up his nose a couple of times in front of the hall mirror, but even that didn't cheer him up.

"I have a feeling," said Willie, "that it's going to be a lousy evening."

Then when we got to William Henry's house, he was missing. This is the way William Henry is all the time. His mother said that he had been waiting for us on the front steps and if we left without him, he'd be brokenhearted. William Henry heals easy, and so we didn't care much about his heart, but Willie was afraid of being taken in hand if we didn't make some effort to help find William Henry. So we looked around outside the house, and finally behind a bush by the front sidewalk we saw this small ghost lying flat on its back with its toes pointing straight up. This had to be William Henry because if you just point a gun at him and say, "Bang!" he thinks he's been shot, and as a result, he spends a good deal of time on his back with his toes pointing straight up. William Henry is so young that he's not all there yet.

Well, William Henry's mother kept trying to bring him to, and Willie and I were getting desperate because it was so late. Then I got an idea and told him he couldn't be shot because he was a ghost and already dead. So he got up right away. But then he slowed us up some more, because when he saw me in my pirate disguise, he had one of his nervous fits, and his mother had to tell him about twenty-five times that it was me. Ordinarily, I'd have been pleased at William Henry's reaction to the way I looked, but he had said that it was Ronald Pruitt who had shot him with a space gun and that Ronald had a fish bowl on his head, which upset Willie and me because if William Henry was right, Ronald was dressed like an astronaut and if we didn't hurry up and get to Mr. Bolger's, Ronald might win the prize.

And that's what happened. We couldn't walk fast because of Willie's big shoes and William Henry's legs, which are only four years old and short. And when we finally got to Mr. Bolger's house, sure enough Ronald had just been awarded the prize, which was a keen pocket watch with an orange cat on the back of the case. He would never have won if Willie and I had got there on time. All the kids said so. They all agreed that Ronald's disguise couldn't hold a candle to ours, but he had the watch and he stood around in his space suit acting as if he had just been to Mars and back. Ronald loves to beat Willie or me out of something.

One good thing though, Mr. Bolger had cider and doughnuts for refreshments and after he'd awarded the prize, he went into his house and left it up to his housekeeper, who is deaf, to bring the refreshments out to the table in the yard where we ate, and without help Ronald couldn't get the glass bowl off to eat. Nobody helped him.

Chapter XV
MORE BAD LUCK

When the food was gone, which happened right before Ronald came back from having Mr. Bolger help him get the glass bowl off, Willie and William Henry and I left to go trick-or-treating. Willie and I usually have a good time on Halloween because everybody admires us, and nobody ever guesses who we are. But this Halloween turned out disgusting all the way round. We were still griping when we left Mr. Bolger's about Ronald getting the prize, and the subject made such an impression on William Henry that from then on all evening, with his talk about prizes, he never let us forget that Ronald had beat us out of a watch. What mind William Henry has is one-track. Besides, everywhere we went William Henry got all the attention just because he is less than three feet tall and his brain is undeveloped.

We went first to Aunt Gertrude's house. Always before, Aunt Gertrude had been a lot of fun to visit on Halloween since she was always impressed with our disguises and never recognized us. But when we rang the doorbell and she opened the door, the first person she saw was William Henry because he started right in. So Aunt Gertrude said, "My goodness, it's a ghost," and with William Henry after her, she ran through the hall to the sitting room.

"Look, John, it's a ghost," she said.

Uncle John, who was watching a news broadcast on television, didn't even look away from the screen. "So it is," he said. After all, everybody knows that ghosts don't giggle and talk like William Henry Winningham.

But all Aunt Gertrude could admire was William Henry, who was chasing her around saying, "Don't be afraid. It's me. It's William Henry." And she kept pretending that she really thought he was a ghost until William Henry caught her and said, "It's really William Henry. I won't hurt you." Then he said, "Don't be afraid of the pirate. It's only Andy. And that's Willie." Willie and I could have killed him. This is what you get for taking a little kid with you who doesn't know how to act.

Aunt Gertrude couldn't exclaim enough over William Henry. "You really take the prize, William Henry," she said. "Doesn't he, John? Doesn't he take the prize?"

Uncle John, who hadn't taken his eyes off a lineup of contestants in a beauty contest, said William Henry certainly did.

Willie lit up his nose several times, and I swung my cutlass around. But it didn't do any good. William Henry was all Aunt Gertrude could talk about. And he was only a ghost. It doesn't take any brains to put on a sheet. While Aunt Gertrude was getting us some cookies and candy to put in our trick-or-treat bags, William Henry kept saying to Willie and me, "I took the prize. Ronald Pruitt didn't take the prize. I took the prize." Willie and I ignored him and watched television with Uncle John, but it doesn't do any good to ignore William Henry because he never knows you're doing it.

"I took the prize, didn't I, Andy? Didn't I, Willie?" he kept saying. "Old Ronald Pruitt didn't take it. Aren't you glad? I took the prize."

Willie's mother might have tried to realize that William Henry would spoil our whole evening. Because everywhere we went, it was the same story. You'd think no one had ever seen a ghost before. And William Henry always told everybody who he was and who we were, even though we kept telling him that he wasn't supposed to. Everywhere we went, William Henry kept saying, "Do I take the prize?" And everybody laughed and said that he certainly did. And we didn't get to go to nearly as many houses as usual because William Henry was always getting behind tables and chairs to boo at people or running away into some other part of the house to hide and make ghost noises. We kept having to wait for him to come back from somewhere. And then all the time we were walking to another house William Henry talked and talked and talked about being a scary ghost and taking the prize. Willie said that William Henry was the most boring conversationalist he'd ever heard. We were really mad at Willie's mother.

You might think that things couldn't get worse. But they did. William Henry suddenly announced when we were at least five blocks from his house that he was tired and he was sleepy and his bag was too heavy and his arm hurt and his feet hurt and he wanted to go home and he couldn't walk any more. So I had to carry him. In the process he knocked my tape loose so that my scar came undone, and that's when I knew that the whole evening was a bust. Willie had to carry all the bags, and he said that it was no wonder William Henry was tired. He said that William Henry's bag weighed about a ton and that everybody must have given him twice as much candy as they had given us. So there we were—me loaded down with William Henry, who was sound asleep from the moment I picked him up, and Willie loaded down with the bags and hardly able to walk in his floppy shoes when the worst thing of all happened. We were robbed.

For suddenly, about a block from William Henry's house, three figures with black handkerchiefs over their noses and chins stepped out of a dark driveway by Jackie Carr's house.

"Stand and deliver," said one of them in this gloomy voice.

"What do you mean?" said Willie. "Get out of the way."

But one of them grabbed Willie from behind, and the other two took the bags.

"Those belong to us," I said. "What do you think you're doing?"

84

"What's the big idea, you big thieves?" said Willie.

"We're robbing the rich to give to the poor," said one of the highwaymen. And they put the bags in their bike baskets and rode away as fast as they could.

"We'll get you," Willie and I yelled. "Just wait. We'll catch you."

We could hear the highwaymen laughing as they rode away. It was one of the most humiliating things that had ever happened to us. We hadn't even been able to put up a fight. I couldn't do anything with William Henry on my hands, asleep and hanging around my neck choking me. And Willie couldn't move fast enough in his big clown shoes.

Well, we delivered William Henry to his mother and told her how we'd been robbed by a gang of highwaymen. William Henry woke up long enough to tell his mother that he'd won all the prizes, but the last we saw of him he was sound asleep again. After that, Willie and I walked around looking for the highwaymen, but we didn't see them again. So finally we went home. It was the worst Halloween we'd ever spent.

Chapter XVI
A TERRIFIC DEDUCTION

The next day, which was Saturday, everybody was talking about the highwaymen. They had held up Freddie Clark, Archie Monroe, Hubert Welsh, Jackie Carr, Morris Somers, Ronald Pruitt, and a whole bunch of other people. And everybody was discovering that articles were missing from their houses. Freddie's watch was gone. Archie said that his mother was turning the house upside down looking for a little silver clock. Old Mrs. Peabody couldn't find a silver paper knife which she always kept on her desk. And when we were eating lunch, Aunt Gertrude called to say that Uncle John's gold watch, which had been his great grandfather's, had disappeared.

"Taking a gold watch is no harmless prank," said my father. "Somebody ought to find out who those little ruffians are before they get into worse trouble."

"What this town obviously needs is two good detectives," I said.

My father looked at me in no uncertain terms. "You are not to get mixed up in any of these shenanigans," he said.

My father gets really tough when it comes to shenanigans. So there we were, Willie and I, with a big case of theft looking us right in the face, and we weren't supposed to get mixed up in it. But Willie and I talked it over, and we came to the conclusion that it was our duty to get mixed up. Somebody had to find out who those little ruffians were before they got into worse trouble.

Since we had to investigate as unnoticeably as possible, we called together Freddie, Archie, Jackie, Hubert, and Morris, and explained our problem and asked them to divide up and go calling all over the neighborhood to make a list of all the people who had articles missing. Then Willie and I went to Aunt Gertrude's. We pretended that we were just making a friendly visit, but what we were really after was a clue to the identity of the highwaymen.

86

There was a possibility that even Aunt Gertrude might have noticed some revealing clue about them which Willie and I had missed in the dark.

But we couldn't ask questions for fear that our fathers would find out we were detecting, and we didn't learn anything helpful. Aunt Gertrude was hunting for Uncle John's watch, and she set us to work helping her. She said that Uncle John insisted he remembered winding the watch and setting it against the time of a sports telecast. But she said that on thinking the matter over, she realized two things: one, she knew Uncle John, and he would lose his head if he could, and two, she knew all the children in the neighborhood, and none of them would steal a watch.

Aunt Gertrude is all right. She makes delicious chocolate fudge cake. But she is easy to fool. As Willie and I knew from past experience, she never recognizes anybody in disguise, and so how could she know what neighborhood anybody was from? So Willie and I left Aunt Gertrude still looking for the watch and went back to our detective agency. Freddie and the others were there with the list of houses that had been robbed.

"How are you going to find out who the thieves are?" said Hubert.

Willie and I couldn't admit it since we had a reputation to think of, but we didn't know what we were going to do. None of the kids had noticed anything helpful about the highwaymen, and of course we couldn't go to the robbed houses and investigate for clues.

"First, Willie and I are going to do some heavy thinking," I said.

"And after that you can count on us to get the loot back," said Willie, "because if anybody can identify and catch those thieves, it's us."

"How can we identify the thieves when we don't even have a clue?" said Willie when the other guys had left.

"And how can we get a clue when we can't ask questions?" I said.

Willie and I were really mad at our fathers.

"What makes me the maddest," said Willie, "is losing those bags without even putting up a fight. If I hadn't had those shoes on, I don't care if there were three of them and that big dog, I would have——"

"Willie!" I said. "There's a clue!"

"Where?" said Willie.

"The dog. Who was that big dog?"

We were really excited. You can't disguise a dog. We sat and thought about all the big dogs we knew.

Then Willie said reluctantly, "I think it was Great-heart Jones."

He was right. As soon as he said it, I knew he was right. And we weren't happy about it, even though we had made a terrific deduction, because now we knew who the highwaymen were. If they had turned out to be some creeps like Perry Swanson or Bertie Pruitt, it would have been all right, but we hated to think that we were going to have to turn Rufus and Dreyfus Jones over to the police.

"Let's give up the case," said Willie. "I don't care if we don't solve it."

At first, I almost agreed with him. Everybody, except mothers, admires Rufus and Dreyfus. They can stay under water longer than anybody else in town. They aren't afraid to do anything. One of the most admirable sights I ever saw was Rufus and Dreyfus riding on their bicycles down Main Street in the middle of traffic. They were standing on their heads at the time. Aunt Gertrude said once that it was a good thing the Jones twins' father is a doctor because their broken bones would bankrupt anybody who wasn't a thief.

So you can see why we didn't want to see Rufus and Dreyfus arrested. But then I thought about Uncle John's great grandfather's watch.

"It seems to me," I told Willie, "that what we have to do is concentrate on the fact that the twins may be robbers and ignore the fact that they are the best high divers in town. We don't have to report Rufus and Dreyfus to the police until we are absolutely sure that they have the loot. I think that we should go to the clubhouse of the Geronimoes and do some detecting."

This plan was so dangerous that Willie agreed right away.

Chapter XVII
ALL TIED UP

The Geronimoes are all in the eighth grade, three years ahead of Willie and me in school. Rufus and Dreyfus are their chiefs, and they have a clubhouse in the woods behind the Jones house. All the Geronimoes are daring, but I had never heard of their doing anything that wasn't ethical. Yet, if our deduction about Greatheart was right, they had to be the highwaymen. So Willie and I headed for the Jones house, which is at the edge of town. We left our bikes in a parking lot beside Dr. Jones's office, climbed a fence at the back, and cut through the woods. It was the middle of a Saturday afternoon, and since the Geronimoes might be in the clubhouse, we thought we'd better approach from the rear. The day was very sunny and quiet, and hot for November. The only sounds Willie and I could hear were woods noises, but we weren't taking any chances. We cautiously circled the clubhouse, and sure enough, there were three bikes parked in the back.

There aren't very many kids our age who would dare to go into the territory of the Geronimoes. And ordinarily even Willie and I wouldn't have gone near the clubhouse when the Geronimoes were in it. The door had at least ten padlocks on it, and there were signs all over the door like "Keep Out," "Danger," "Trespassers Persecuted," "Headshrinking Done Here," "Beware. We See You," and various other warnings. But when we're out detecting, Willie and I don't let anything stop us, no matter how scared we are. We crawled on our stomachs up to the little window at the back of the house, stood up, peeped in, and got the shock of our lives.

The first thing I saw was Uncle John's great grandfather's watch. The loot was scattered all over a table in the middle of the room, and there beside the table looking at the loot and talking were Rufus Jones and Teddie Simpkins and Michael Antonelli. And the next thing I saw was Greatheart coming out from under the table and barking at the window. Willie and I dodged out of sight, but not fast enough. The Geronimoes had whirled around and seen us, and as we took off through the woods, we heard their war whoop, which is enough to lift your hair off your head all by itself.

Willie said later that if anybody'd had a stop watch on us, he bet we'd have the speed record for kids our age. With the Geronimoes yelling like that and being robbers, they weren't like anyone we'd ever known, and we were running for our lives. Even though they were three years older than us and bigger, we almost got away, but all of a sudden the yell started up ahead of us. Dreyfus and Alex Yeardley were approaching from the front. Willie and I didn't have a chance. We veered to the right and jumped a little creek, but then this bloodcurdling yell began to sound on all sides of us. They had us surrounded, and then they closed in. We put up a good fight, but the Geronimoes got us down, tied us up, and carried us off to their clubhouse. All this time they never said a word. They just made these terrible whooping sounds. It was enough to freeze your blood solid.

In the clubhouse they wound ropes around our chests and tied us to a chair. Then they stood in a circle around the chairs and stared at us with their arms folded. They didn't talk. They just looked. If it hadn't been for Greatheart, who kept walking back and forth between the Geronimoes and us, acting as if everybody was friends, I would probably have died. Dogs are always comfortable to have around. But even so, Willie said later that he thought his time had come. So they stared at us and stared at us, and finally about the time I thought I couldn't stand it any longer, Rufus said to Willie, who was white as a sheet, "You, Paleface, why are you here?"

"To be scalped?" said Willie.

"Why were you trespassing on the territory of the Geronimoes?" Rufus said to me.

"We're detectives," I said, "detecting. We recognized Greatheart last night." Greatheart put his head on my knees and stared at me, too.

"They're not so dumb," said Teddie Simpkins. "Maybe they are the ones."

"I still say they aren't the ones," said Rufus.

Willie rolled his eyes at me. It sounded as though the Geronimoes were cracking up. I took hold of Greatheart's collar.

"We came to get the bags you took from us last night," I said.

"Is a little candy so important?" said Dreyfus.

"It was our candy," said Willie.

"Besides," I said, hanging onto Greatheart, "we're investigating you. We're looking for certain missing objects."

"If they knew the stuff was in the bag," said Teddie, "they're the ones who stole it."

"Us!" said Willie, forgetting that he was tied up in Geronimo territory. "We're detectives. We catch thieves. And there's the loot right there on the table. We're going to report you to the police."

"You're nuts," said Mike Antonelli.

"Wait a minute," said Rufus. "Let's get to the bottom

of this," said Dreyfus. "Now, Andy and Willie, I can't believe that you are thieves," said Rufus. "But those objects were either in one of the bags we took from you or in the bag we took from Ronald Pruitt," said Dreyfus. "We didn't steal those things," said Rufus. "So what's your explanation?" said Dreyfus.

"Ronald Pruitt," said Willie. "We might have known. When you get to the bottom of something, you always find Ronald Pruitt."

"I think they're innocent," said Rufus.

"They could be passing the buck," said Teddie. "It's got to be them or Ronald."

"Why?" I said. "You took a lot of bags."

"We were organized," said Alex. "Yours and Ronald's were the last ones collected. The others had already been delivered."

"Don't talk too much," said Dreyfus.

"You guys sound suspicious to me," I said. "After all, you have the loot. How do we know you didn't take it?"

"Yeah, how do we know?" said Willie. "You took our candy. That's stealing. And it's not ethical."

The Geronimoes looked embarrassed.

"Tell them," said Alex. "I don't want anybody thinking I'm a thief."

So then Dreyfus told us about this boy who lived out in the country and how he never had any fun because he'd been sick in bed for a long time and how when they'd gone with their father to see him, they'd told him in private that the Geronimoes would remember him on Halloween.

93

And so they had organized a redistribution plan so that the treats would go to a deserving person who couldn't have the fun of going trick or treating on Halloween.

"We'd carried out seven sacks of candy," said Rufus, "when Dreyfus and Mike and Alex brought in the last ones from you and Ronald Pruitt to the clubhouse for Teddie and me to deliver. And that's when we found the gold watch and other stuff. We've been trying to figure out how to find out who the thief was and how to return the stolen goods without getting involved."

"Imagine Ronald behind bars," said Willie. "It's about time."

Rufus looked at us. "I'm satisfied that they didn't do it," he said to the others. All the Geronimoes nodded.

"Can we count on you to return this stuff without involving us?" said Dreyfus.

We said that they could. So the Geronimoes untied us, and Dreyfus gathered up all the stolen things and put them into a paper sack. Then he said, "By the way, after we left you last night, we got to thinking that taking candy from babies like William Henry wasn't part of our redistribution plan. So we left one bag there by the door when we brought the last four bags in. We were going to put it on William Henry's porch as soon as we'd taken the other bags out to the country, but after we found the stolen articles, we forgot about it. You can see that William Henry gets his candy back."

So then they made Willie and me swear on our honor as detectives not to reveal the secret of the Geronimoes' redistribution plan and not to report Ronald to the police.

"We'll take care of Ronald," said Dreyfus.

"And if you break your word," said Rufus, "the vengeance of the Geronimoes will fall on you, too."

"I'd hate to be in Ronald Pruitt's shoes," said Willie as we were on the way home.

I felt the same way. There was no telling what the Geronimoes would do to him. Willie thought that maybe they'd bury Ronald in an ant hill. But I thought it was too late in the year for ants.

Chapter XVIII
AN UNBELIEVABLE MYSTERY

Willie and I returned the stolen articles to their owners right away. We called Freddie, Archie, Jackie, Morris, and Hubert together and told them that we'd recovered the loot, though we couldn't tell how because innocent people were involved, and after we'd received their congratulations, we organized a redistribution plan. Archie, Jackie, Morris, and Willie rang front door bells and made conversation while Freddie and Hubert and I slipped in through the back door and returned the stolen item. If the back door was locked, we all paid a visit and created an interesting distraction so that one of us would have a chance to hide the missing article on the premises. It was a lot of fun. Freddie hid old Mrs. Peabody's paper knife in a dictionary. I bet she never did find it. Freddie hid it in the *p*'s for Peabody paper knife.

But the case wasn't over yet. The unbelievable thing came later.

It turned out that William Henry had stayed in his house all day because he'd heard that there was a thief in town and he was afraid that he'd be stolen. So we sent Jackie and Morris to find the trick-or-treat bag on William Henry's porch accidentally and deliver it to him. I suppose that when William Henry got his candy back, he decided there wasn't any thief, he's so dumb, because about fifteen minutes later when Willie and I were sitting on my steps wondering how Ronald would look scalped, along came William Henry with the bag. His mouth was full of candy, and he was all smiles.

"Look at my prize," he said. "I took the prize."

"Good night," said Willie, "do we have to go through all that again? Go somewhere else, William Henry."

"See?" said William Henry, holding up a watch. "See my prize? I took the prize. Ronald didn't take the prize."

Willie and I looked at it with our mouths open. It was the watch Ronald had won at Mr. Bolger's party.

"Where did you get that?" I said.

"In my trick-or-treat bag," said William Henry. "I took the prize, didn't I?"

Willie and I looked at each other. We had both figured out the same thing at the same time. If William Henry had Ronald's watch, then it wasn't Ronald's bag that had had the loot in it.

"Ronald isn't the one?" said Willie.

"How could he be?" I said.

"Do you think we'd better tell the Geronimoes," said Willie, "before they skin Ronald or whatever they're going to do to him?"

I hated to, partly because Ronald just naturally has a skinning coming and partly because the Geronimoes might start suspecting us again, but it was the only ethical thing to do. So we rode back to the clubhouse. Nobody was there. We found out later that the Geronimoes had gone looking for Ronald and had found him in the act of teasing Caesar Bolger, Mr. Bolger's dog. Ronald was teasing Caesar through Mr. Bolger's fence, of course. He's always teasing dogs when they are tied up or otherwise can't get at him. Anyway, when the Geronimoes surrounded him, Ronald was scared, but when they accused him of being a thief, Ronald got some of his nerve back. He said that he wasn't a thief, but somebody was, because somebody had stolen his trick-or-treat bag and his watch, too. He was so angry about it that he shook the Geronimoes, and they decided not to punish him for robbing people until they were sure he had. So they gave him a good paddling for teasing dogs.

When Willie and I finally found Rufus and Dreyfus, we told them why Ronald couldn't have been the thief. Rufus and Dreyfus got interested in the news that Ronald had won a pocket watch at Mr. Bolger's party. So we explained how it had happened and how Ronald wouldn't have won if we'd got to the party on time. We were telling what a disgusting Halloween we'd had and what a pain in the neck William Henry had been with all his talk about prizes when all of a sudden Rufus and Dreyfus began to laugh and hit each other on the back. Then they hit Willie and me on the back, said we were good kids, jumped on their bikes, and rode away yelling their Geronimo war whoop. Rufus and Dreyfus aren't like anybody else. They are unusual and great.

Well, that's about all there is to tell about the case of the mysterious Halloween thief. When we told William Henry that he had Ronald Pruitt's watch and should give it back, William Henry had broken the watch and didn't care about it any more, anyway. So he left it on Ronald's doorstep. The crystal was broken and one of the hands was gone and the face was scratched and some little springs were sticking out. Ronald was really burned up, but he shouldn't have won that prize in the first place.

To this day Willie and I are stumped when we think about this case. We made a good deduction about Great-heart and about Ronald's not being the thief, but nobody knows yet who the thief was. The Geronimoes must have been mixed up about the bags. Because if they're right, it doesn't make sense. Ronald wasn't the thief. And it certainly wasn't Willie and me. So who else could it have been? Willie says that if the Geronimoes are right, the thief must have been a ghost.

Chapter XIX
RONALD MAKES AN ACCUSATION

Of all of Willie's and my early big cases, Willie's favorite was the fifth one because that's when the general public began to realize how safe they are with Willie and me around. Actually, what we call our fifth big case was two cases, but since one of them solved the other, Willie and I always think of them together.

It all began one afternoon about a week after Halloween. Ronald Pruitt on his way home from school came across William Henry Winningham trying to rake Mrs. Peabody's leaves. Since Ronald never misses a chance to tease a little kid who is unprotected, he started growling at William Henry from behind a tree and saying that he was a lion loose from a zoo. Ronald is loose from a zoo, all right, but William Henry, who believes everything anybody tells him, believed the lion part, too. He was just on the verge of going into one of his fits when Jackie Carr's little sister came around the house and heard Ronald. Since nobody ever bothers William Henry when Jackie's little sister is present, Ronald started to leave. But Jackie's little sister got in front of him, stuck out her arm full length at him, and said, "I warned you, Ronald Pruitt. I warned you to leave William Henry alone. Now you'd better look out. Something is going to happen to you."

Hubert Welsh saw the whole thing. He said it sent a chill clear up his backbone because Ronald hadn't walked twenty feet across the grass at the side of Mrs. Peabody's house when a dead limb fell off a tree and missed Ronald by about one-half inch. Ronald looked over his shoulder at Jackie's little sister and then started running. He ran all the way home, and the next day at school he said Jackie's little sister was a witch because she could look into the future and make things happen to a person.

At first, Jackie's little sister, who likes being in the public eye, didn't mind being a witch. But a day or so later when Willie and I went after school to our detective

99

agency, we found her there waiting to hire us to detect that she wasn't a witch. Actually, we found her waiting for us on top of my father's car to avoid Mr. Bolger's dog Caesar, who was walking around the car trying to get to her. Most of the kids, even Jackie's little sister, were afraid of Caesar because the summer before, Edgar Bolger had told everybody that Caesar was a killer. At that time, I couldn't understand the stories Edgar told about Caesar. It had always seemed to me that you couldn't find a friendlier dog. Caesar had always struck me as the type who was so glad to see you that he knocked you down. Anyway, after we had taken Caesar home and shut the gate on him, Jackie's little sister came down and told us why she was there.

It seemed that she had been hanging upside down from a tree limb in order to entertain William Henry. But suddenly he had turned white.

"You're a witch," he said. "You're a wicked witch."

And he had run home as if the bogeyman were after him. And every time Jackie's little sister tried to talk to him, he went into one of his fits. So that's why she had come to hire Willie and me. She said that if we detected that she wasn't a witch, William Henry would be convinced.

Willie and I liked the idea of having Jackie's little sister for a customer because she is one of the most solvent persons we know. But the case looked too clear-cut. That is, if looking into the future made her a witch, then she was a witch. But then we got to thinking that maybe it was just lucky that the tree limb almost killed Ronald and that we should investigate her looking-into-the-future ability. So we told her that we'd take the case. And we told her to look into the future again and that while she was about it, she might as well see something good for Willie and me and anybody else whose welfare she was interested in.

So she looked. Then she announced that within a week Willie and I were going to get our names in the paper for solving a big case, within twenty-four hours William Henry was going to get a pony, and within four hours she was going to get a raise in her allowance. And after Willie and I had posted her predictions on a tree in front of my house, there was nothing to do but wait.

To pass the time while we waited, we rode our bikes down to look at the public enemies. Willie and I are in the habit of studying the Wanted posters on the bulletin board at the post office so we'll be ready in case someone who is wanted comes to town. There was a new poster up about a thief named Howard G. Trillinger. He had a little black mustache and a bunch of aliases. As soon as I saw the picture, I got the feeling that I'd seen him somewhere. Right away, Willie got the same feeling.

"It's that new dentist," said Willie, "that Doctor Truesdale."

You can always count on Willie to have an eye for faces. It was Dr. Truesdale I'd been thinking of without knowing it.

"Howard G. Trillinger has another alias," said Willie.

At first, we thought we'd better go straight to the police station with our information. But ever since Willie and I had gone into the detecting business, we'd tried to help the police and they didn't seem to appreciate it. The last suspicious character we had reported had turned out to be the police chief's uncle in Wakanda for a visit. Considering his looks, I still say it was an understandable mistake, but the police chief didn't see it that way. So under the circumstances, we decided to make absolutely sure about Howard G. Trillinger.

The obvious move was for one of us to go to have our teeth looked at so that we could see Dr. Truesdale close up. And it turned out that Willie was the ideal one to go, since when we checked our teeth, I had what looked like a little cavity, but Willie's teeth looked perfect. So we went to Willie's house, and Willie began to complain to his mother about the miserable condition of his teeth and about not wanting to have teeth like old Mr. Hennington, who didn't have any.

Willie's mother was quite surprised. She looked all over the inside of Willie's mouth. "I don't see anything wrong with your teeth, Willie," she said.

Willie pulled his cheek way over to one side. "Look there," he said. "Look at the back sides of my back teeth. Do you call that nothing wrong?"

Since Willie's mother couldn't see the back sides of his back teeth, she began to get convinced. "I'll make an appointment with Doctor Yeardley right away," she said.

"By the time I can get in to see him," said Willie, "my teeth will be gone. Why don't you call that new dentist? He can probably see me right away in time to save whatever is left."

Well, Willie's mother was in such a state of shock over Willie's wanting to go to a dentist that she called Dr. Truesdale and got Willie an appointment for the very next day after school.

Maybe it looks as if Willie and I already had our hands full proving that Jackie's little sister wasn't a witch. But Howard G. Trillinger was a public enemy, and we figured that if we didn't expose Dr. Truesdale right away, there was no telling what might happen. We thought we'd have Jackie's little sister's case settled satisfactorily pretty soon anyway, because when we went to check on the situation after Willie had got his appointment arranged, it looked as if she couldn't lose. As soon as William Henry had found out that she'd seen a pony in his future, he'd started liking her again. And besides, Jackie's little sister had got so interested in the possibilities opening up for witches that she was listing other events she was going to see in the future, like William Henry winning a contest and all the kids, except Ronald, getting a trip to the moon. Everybody, except Ronald, said that it was great to have a witch right in our own neighborhood.

Chapter XX

WILLIE AND I MAKE AN ACCUSATION

But twenty-four hours later our detecting in both cases hadn't got us anywhere, though it wasn't our fault. First, Willie went to the dentist, and when he came out into the waiting room, I could see that he was shaken up. He'd expected Dr. Truesdale just to look over his perfect teeth, but it turned out they weren't. And just as Dr. Truesdale had picked up the grinder, Willie remembered that the posters always said, "This man is armed and dangerous." Willie said he aged ten years. The dentist's assistant kept mopping him off, and Dr. Truesdale kept telling him it wouldn't hurt at all. But Willie said that it was the most nerve-racking experience of his life.

"What about Doctor Truesdale?" I said.

"There's no doubt in my mind that he's a public enemy," said Willie.

I had got a good look at him myself. He was the right height, and his hair and eyes were brown just as the poster said. His eyeglasses weren't in the statistics, but of course they could be part of the alias. Willie said that Dr. Truesdale should have shaved off that little mustache because it was a dead giveaway. We got on our bikes and went straight to the police station.

Since we'd had some trouble getting in to see the Chief of Police the last two or three times we'd gone to confer with him, we didn't waste any time shooting past the desk of Officer Toomey and into the office of the Chief. I thought our news had better be kept quiet to avoid a public panic. So I went up to his desk and leaned across and whispered, "Howard G. Trillinger is in town."

"Who?" he said.

"Howard G. Trillinger. He's on the Wanted poster at the post office."

"What about him?" said the Chief.

"He's in town," I said. "Right here in Wakanda. The FBI wants him."

"He's under an alias," said Willie. "He's calling himself Doctor Truesdale."

Mr. Toomey, who had followed us, made a funny noise. He probably couldn't believe his ears. The Chief just looked at us. We thought at first that he was stunned at the news of our discovery. But then he practically surprised Willie and me to death the way he took it.

"Now listen to me, Andy and Willie," he said. "Howard G. Trillinger, or whatever his name is, is not in this town. You can take my word for it. And I'm asking you for the last time to forget this detective business before you cause yourselves or someone else trouble."

"You should listen to him," said Mr. Toomey, escorting us out. He was grinning. There are always some people who like to hear you get bawled out.

"Well," said Willie, when we were outside, "there's cooperation for you."

"It's funny," I said. "We've got one case on our hands because Ronald makes an accusation and everybody listens. And now we've got another because we make an accusation and nobody listens."

"What makes his accusation better than our accusation?" said Willie. "His probably isn't even true. And it certainly isn't official."

Then when we got home, we found that our other case was in even worse shape. Jackie's little sister hadn't got a raise in her allowance, and now the twenty-four hours were just up and William Henry hadn't got the pony. You might think that at least we'd solved the case and detected that Jackie's little sister wasn't a witch. But Ronald had told all the kids that now it was more obvious than ever that she was, because witches aren't able to see good things in the future. And when William Henry didn't get his pony, he said that Jackie's little sister was an old witch.

So Willie and I got this idea that we thought was

quite tricky. We posted a prediction on the tree that Ronald would immediately get a terrible stomachache which would last three days. The tricky part was that it was Willie and me looking into Ronald's future, although everybody would just naturally suppose that it was Jackie's little sister. Since Willie and I weren't witches, the bad prediction wouldn't come true, and this way we would be getting Jackie's little sister off the hook and giving ourselves time to solve the case. A person needs time to investigate scientifically whether someone is a witch or not. And besides we had this other case demanding our attention, too. Since the Chief didn't know that Howard G. Trillinger was in town, it seemed more obvious than ever that he was. We'd decided to notify the FBI, and we had to keep an eye on Dr. Truesdale until the government agents came to pick him up. And besides needing time, we figured that the prediction was the least we could do for Jackie's little sister, since our detecting so far had made things worse for her, what with Ronald Pruitt coming up with all this information about witches that nobody else had.

But the surprising thing was that as soon as Ronald read the prediction, he started having stabbing pains in his stomach. He doubled up, and he moaned, and when we saw that his suffering was turning all the kids against our client even more, we had to tell the facts, even though everybody might say we were witches. So I explained that it was Willie's and my prediction. And we told Ronald just to try calling *us* names. But then Ronald said that he'd already guessed that Jackie's little sister hadn't done the predicting because his pains were easing off.

"You and Willie," said Ronald, "aren't any better at predicting than you are at detecting."

Willie had already put up with a grinder and a public enemy and the Chief that afternoon, and Ronald Pruitt was just too much. So Willie said that we were as good at looking into the future as anybody else. And he was all for catching Ronald and giving him some pains in the stomach.

"We'll show him," said Willie to me, "who is a predictor and who isn't."

Ordinarily, I would have been all for it. But our class at school was going on an educational trip to Chicago the next day. I had been looking forward to this trip for a long time, and if I did anything to Ronald, my parents would probably crack down on me and not let me go on the trip. My parents are hardly ever on my side. So Willie and I decided to make a true prediction about Ronald's stomach after the trip.

Chapter XXI
A HUNCH AND A PREDICTION

It was a bad time to be leaving town right when we had two difficult cases on our hands. But we needed to do some heavy thinking anyway, and we could do that anywhere. We planned to spend our spare time on the trip deciding what a thief like Howard G. Trillinger was after in Wakanda and also what to do to detect a witch. And we were going to exchange ideas the first chance we got.

But we didn't have time to talk until we were on the train going home. Miss Easter had us all seated facing forward on one side of the aisle. Willie and I were sitting together, but even so we couldn't talk about our cases. Betsy Miller and Agatha Crawley were sitting in front of us, and Agatha has the kind of ears that hear everything. So we traveled along for a half hour or so with me thinking and Willie stamping everything with his rubber stamp, which had the initials W. P. on it. He stamped his shirt and the soles of his shoes, and then he opened his shirt and stamped his chest and stomach.

"What are you doing that for?" I said. "Nobody can see those initials."

"If there's a wreck on the way home," said Willie, "and my face is mutilated, they'll be able to identify me by my initials."

Willie thinks of everything. Besides, he'd got this ink pad and stamp for his birthday about three weeks before, and he was crazy about stamping his initials everywhere. Personally, I suspected that Willie's new habit of leaving his initials around was the main reason the Chief had turned against us, because one day when we went to see him and he left his office for a minute, Willie stamped W. P. on everything on the Chief's desk. And when the Chief came back and saw the initials, you'd have thought that Willie had committed a federal crime.

So anyway, we rode along, Willie stamping and me thinking. First, I thought about the witch case and how complicated it was getting, what with Jackie's little sister being a witch because the pains in Ronald's stomach eased off, and then I thought about the public enemy case and how complicated it was getting, what with Dr. Truesdale obviously being Howard G. Trillinger because Howard G. Trillinger would naturally be under an alias. Then the two cases got all mixed up in my head, and I got Dr. Truesdale connected with witches and Jackie Carr's little sister with public enemies. This was crazy. Dr. Truesdale obviously wasn't a witch, and Jackie's little sister obviously wasn't a public enemy. What Willie and I needed to do was some talking so that we could keep the two cases separated and straighten things out one at a time.

The teachers, who were sitting together at the front of the car, weren't paying any attention to us, now that they had us all lined up and on our way home. And I noticed that the only class members behind us were Jackie Carr, who was asleep, and Freddie Clark. So motioning Willie to follow me, I got down on my hands and knees and started crawling toward the back of the car. Freddie saw us go by, but they could dump a load of bricks on Freddie Clark, and he wouldn't squeal. We crawled along looking for another empty seat, and finally at the back of the car we found one facing a seat where a man was stretched out asleep with a newspaper over his face.

"Now," I said, "we can talk. But don't use the name of you-know-who—H. G. T."

"OK," said Willie, who had got out his ink pad and stamp again and was putting W. P. on the back of each hand.

"The first thing we have to figure out," I said, "is what he is after in our town."

"I don't see how we can," said Willie, stamping the window sill. "We don't know everything that's there."

"Well, I've thought of one thing. Mr. Bolger's rare book."

"What rare book?" said Willie, stamping the window.

I swore Willie to secrecy, and then I told him what Edgar Bolger had told Freddie and me the summer before. A man had offered Mr. Bolger ten thousand dollars for this book because this famous author had written remarks about his own book in the margin in various places.

"What's so great about that?" said Willie.

"I don't know," I said. "But Edgar called it a book collector's item, and he should know since his father is a book collector."

"Why would anyone want to steal a book when he could steal a horse or a diamond or something interesting?" said Willie.

"How about those books we saw today in the museum?" I said. "Miss Easter said that they were priceless."

"That's because they were illustrated by old monks," said Willie, looking around for something else to stamp his initials on.

"How do we know that this famous author wasn't an old monk?" I said.

The more I thought about it, the bigger hunch I had that this book of Mr. Bolger's was what the public enemy was after. But Willie, who was still concentrating more on stamping everything in sight than on our problem, wasn't convinced that a book could attract a thief. So I told him how Edgar had taken Freddie and me to see the book and how just after he had showed us an autograph to Mr. Bolger in the front and was starting to show us the writing in the margin, we had to run because Edgar heard his grandfather coming. At this, Willie got interested. If you have to run to keep grown-ups from knowing you know something, it's important.

"How did Edgar find out about the book?" said Willie.

"He heard his father tell his grandfather that he shouldn't leave something so valuable right there on the hall table where anybody could pick it up. But Mr. Bolger said that at the most a person would just notice an autographed book, and the autograph wasn't valuable."

"Well, it seems to me he's taking a chance," Willie said.

I agreed. And as I told Willie, Freddie and I had been saying just the Saturday before, when we went to deliver a newspaper to Mr. Bolger, that it would be easy for a thief to steal the book, especially on a Saturday night, since Mr. Bolger always goes as regular as clockwork at seventy-thirty to play chess with Jackie Carr's grandfather and since Mr. Bolger's housekeeper is deaf and since Mr. Bolger doesn't lock his front door.

"It's a good thing you and Freddie are honest," said Willie.

And at that moment Miss Easter turned up and made us go back to our seats. Ronald had reported that we were missing. No one is safe with Ronald Pruitt around.

We got home at five o'clock and found Jackie's little sister waiting for us. She said that William Henry had accused her of giving people stomachaches, and she was so mad at Ronald that she had looked into his future and made a list of predictions which she wanted us to write down and post about him: 1) Ronald would get mumps by Monday; 2) Ronald would be bitten by a rattlesnake by Tuesday; 3) Ronald would be stepped on by an elephant by Wednesday. She had us add that he wouldn't be really hurt, only squashed in a little here and there. We posted it because this was certainly one good way to solve the witch case, though as things turned out, it wasn't necessary.

We'd made plans concerning the public enemy case, too, and so at seven o'clock that night Willie and I met and parked our bikes in the alley behind Mr. Bolger's house. Willie had got permission to spend the night with me, and I had got permission to spend the night with him. What we hadn't mentioned was where. We had decided to keep watch over Mr. Bolger's property while he was out that night, and if we had to chase Howard G. Trillinger, we couldn't have our parents spoiling everything by chasing after us.

Chapter XXII
CAUGHT IN THE ACT

Willie and I sneaked through Mr. Bolger's side gate and crawled behind the shrubbery around to some bushes near the path to the front door. At seven-thirty exactly, by the town clock, Mr. Bolger came out of the house and went away down the street. After the sound of his steps died away, everything got quiet. There was a big, white moon coming up over in the direction of Big Walnut Creek, but otherwise there wasn't much going on. We waited and waited and waited. It got dull, what with nothing happening except the moon shining and the leaves rustling and the trees creaking. And it got colder and colder there in the bushes. Willie and I hadn't counted on everything being so cold and lonesome, and if it hadn't been for the kind of detectives we are, I doubt that we could have stood it so long. But it's a good thing we did.

For just as I was getting ready to suggest to Willie that we go to my house and say that we'd decided to spend the night there, somebody lifted the latch on Mr. Bolger's front gate. Willie, who sometimes gives me a pain thinking he has to point out the obvious, jammed his sharpest elbow in my ribs to be sure I noticed. A man was going up the path and onto the porch and through the door. We hardly had time to realize we'd seen somebody when there he was coming out. Apparently, he left the door ajar, because just as he came down the steps, Caesar galloped out of the house and jumped at the man to knock him down in his friendly way. But the man hit Caesar a whack on the head. And the next thing we knew, the path was empty except for old Caesar lying at the foot of the steps.

It was a queer thing. Willie and I were waiting in the bushes because we expected a thief. But somehow when a real thief really came, nothing seemed real. For a minute we couldn't believe it all had happened. And we were scared. But then we heard Caesar groan, and we got mad. Nobody hits a friend of ours on the head and gets away with it. So Willie ran to get Mr. Bolger, and I jumped on my bike and set out in the direction the thief had taken. I caught sight of him right away. He was walking fast, always down the shadiest streets, and once he slipped down an alley. But all the guys in our neighborhood had played this game. I did a first-class job of shadowing and followed him all the way to Main Street and saw him go into the Crawley Hotel.

Then I went back to get Willie. Mr. Bolger had carried Caesar into the house, and he and Jackie Carr's grandfather were giving Caesar first aid. Mr. Bolger at that point was more interested in the bump on Caesar's head than he was in how it got there. Besides, he hadn't noticed, as I had, that the book was missing. So Willie and I didn't take time for explanations. We thought that by the time everything was explained and the police got moving, the thief might have got away. So since Caesar was showing signs of life, Willie and I left.

"It wasn't Howard G. Trillinger," said Willie. "I could see him well enough to see that he didn't have a mustache. Besides, he was too little."

"It was an accomplice," I said. "We should have expected an accomplice. He and Howard G. Trillinger are meeting at Crawley's hotel."

In *Big City Detective* on television, crooks are always meeting in hotels to plot and to divide the loot, and the detective always catches them in the act. We figured that if we could catch Howard G. Trillinger and the accomplice in the act and get our hands on the book, we'd have the evidence, and then the Chief would have to listen to us.

We were glad to see Mr. McGregor standing in front of the hotel because we thought he might come in handy as soon as we got the evidence. Mr. McGregor is a really tough policeman. He's especially tough if you're out after curfew. So we parked our bikes around the corner and ducked into the hotel through a side door. The first person we saw was Tim O'Brien, who worked in the hotel on weekends.

"Is there a stranger staying here?" I asked.

"Sure," said Tim. "Why? What are you doing here?"

"A thin little man," said Willie.

"Mean-looking. Carrying a briefcase," I said.

"That's the man in three hundred eleven," said Tim, "if he hasn't checked out by now. From some questions he asked me, I think he's leaving on the nine o'clock train. What about him?"

"We just wondered," I said, starting up the stairs with Willie right behind.

"Hold on," said Tim. "What is this? Wait a minute."

But by the time Tim finished yelling at us, we were almost up to the second floor. He apparently couldn't decide whether to follow us or go on with his job of mopping the floor, and before he decided, we were out of sight. We found 311 at the end of one wing of the hall around the corner from the elevator. The light was on, but when we leaned against the door and listened, we couldn't hear a sound. I squatted down and was trying to look through the keyhole when suddenly somewhere behind us a voice said, "What do you think you're doing?"

Willie and I whirled around and there coming around the corner from the elevator was the accomplice. He grabbed me by the arm. "I asked you a question," he said, and exactly like a crook in *Big City Detective*, he twisted my arm behind me so that I couldn't think of anything else, let alone a good answer.

"Let go of him," said Willie, trying to pull me loose.

The accomplice gave Willie such a shove that Willie went flying down the corridor backwards, hit a wastebasket in the hall about three doors away, fell over it, and went rolling across the floor. At this moment, Tim and Mr. McGregor came around the corner of the corridor and saw Willie on the floor and me having my arm shoved clear up to my neck bone behind.

"What's going on here?" said Mr. McGregor.

The accomplice tried to look likable. "I've been having a little trouble with these kids," he said. "I caught them trying to break into my room."

"We hadn't started to break in yet," said Willie. "We were listening at his door to see whether he was turning over the loot."

"The loot?" said Mr. McGregor.

"He's a thief," I said. "He hit Mr. Bolger's dog on the head and took Mr. Bolger's rare book. Just ask Mr. Bolger."

At this moment Willie let out such a yell that everybody jumped. "Look," he said. "It's Mr. Bolger's book. It's got his name in it. It was in the wastebasket."

If Mr. McGregor watched *Big City Detective*, he'd have known that at this point he was supposed to drag the thief off to jail whining. But instead he looked as if he couldn't make up his mind what to do. And for a crook caught in the act, I never saw anybody look so confident as that accomplice.

"It's a collector's item," I said. "And he stole it. We saw him."

"He carried it out of Mr. Bolger's house in a briefcase," said Willie. "At least, he was carrying a briefcase when he broke into Mr. Bolger's house. We saw him."

Mr. McGregor had the man open his door, and he found a briefcase in the accomplice's room.

"What'd we tell you?" Willie kept saying. "We told you."

"Be still, Willie," said Mr. McGregor. "We'll all step over to the station and get this thing straightened out."

The accomplice said something about catching a train, but he didn't protest much. It was funny. He didn't seem to realize that Willie and I had caught him in the act. We all went across the street to the police station.

Chapter XXIII
"BLESSED ARE THE PEACEMAKERS"

Willie and I were all smiles when we went into the station. We expected the Chief to admire us at last. But he got this expression as if we were locusts and he had a wheat crop. And for a minute it looked as if he was going to call our parents before he'd even found out why we were there. I couldn't imagine anything worse than my father getting the news that I was at the police station. He's never been able to see me as a detective.

But Mr. McGregor started explaining what had happened, and I was relieved to see the Chief put the phone back and listen. Mr. McGregor reported everything we'd said. Mr. Toomey got the thief's name, which was Schmidt, and some other information and went into the next room. The Chief looked at Mr. Schmidt and Willie and me. He seemed tougher at night than in the daytime, and for some reason I felt a little nervous, even though he and I were on the same side.

"What makes you think that anyone would steal this book?" said the Chief to Willie and me.

"We saw him steal it," said Willie.

"It's worth ten thousand dollars," I said.

Mr. Schmidt laughed.

"He's an accomplice of Howard G. Trillinger," said Willie.

It was immediately clear that this remark was a mistake. So Willie, who is always a quick thinker, said, "I charge this man with assault and battery." And he added, "That means he knocked me down and twisted Andy's arm."

I added, "The book is valuable because of the handwriting in the margins. Edgar Bolger said so. Look at the writing."

Mr. Schmidt laughed again. The Chief stared at him. It was obvious that even if the Chief was against Willie and me, he wasn't going to show any favoritism. He opened the book and looked all through it. Willie beamed at me. "What did we tell you?" he said to the Chief.

"There isn't any writing in the margins of this book," the Chief said.

For a minute I couldn't believe my ears, and Willie looked as if the Chief was speaking a foreign language. Then all of a sudden it flashed on me that Edgar had also said that Caesar was a killer. It was one of the blackest moments of my detective career. I had got Willie into this, and besides I realized that now, what with Willie and me believing and repeating Edgar's big fib, the Chief wouldn't believe any part of our story.

"Now," said Mr. Schmidt, "that you see what liars these kids are, maybe I can go?"

The Chief looked at Willie and me. We couldn't even defend ourselves. What was the use?

But I said, "I'm the one who believed Edgar, and then I convinced Willie."

"And we're not liars," said Willie.

Mr. Schmidt got up.

"Not so fast," said the Chief, picking up the telephone. "Sit down." He called up Mr. Bolger and asked some questions about Caesar and the book. As he hung up, Mr. Toomey came in and said something to the Chief, who looked at Mr. Schmidt. Then he looked at Willie and me. It was all very deliberate and nerve-racking. I couldn't tell who he was going to kill.

"So you've been in this kind of trouble before," he said.

"Me?" said Willie, swallowing.

"When did you come here?" said the Chief to Mr. Schmidt. "What's your business here?"

Mr. Schmidt had stopped trying to look likable. "I got sick on the train this afternoon," he said, "and decided to cut my trip short and go back to Chicago as soon as I could. I've never been in this town before, I don't know anybody here, and I don't know what this is all about." He muttered something I couldn't hear about kids and cops.

The Chief just looked at him. Having somebody just look at you without saying anything makes you very uneasy, and the Chief has the technique down pat. I never saw anybody do more looking and staring than the Chief did that night.

"Look," said Mr. Schmidt, "like I said, I caught these kids trying to break into my hotel room. So I roughed them up a little. I didn't hurt them. And you can see what they're like."

"Yes," said the Chief, "I can see."

I wished I was home in bed. The Chief sat there for a while frowning. Then something about Mr. Schmidt's briefcase, which was lying on his desk, seemed to catch his attention. He stared at it as if he were thinking. Then he looked around all over his desk and stared at the briefcase again. Swinging his swivel chair around so that his back was to us, he said something to Mr. Toomey. Once I thought I heard Mr. Toomey chuckle, and for a moment I hoped that I was wrong about this feeling of danger, but then they turned around, and the Chief fixed this eye on us like a cross between a killer shark and the grade school principal. I wished my father was there.

"So you're the detectives who kept coming here to report what you called suspicious characters and who wouldn't listen to anything we said to you," said the Chief.

"That's it," said Mr. Schmidt. "They cooked the whole thing up."

"You wouldn't listen when we told you that this Trillinger person was not in Wakanda."

"They're crazy," said Mr. Schmidt.

What the Chief said next I can't remember exactly. I was so sure that Willie and I were going to be sent to prison for not listening that I was too scared to concentrate on what the Chief was saying. But I do remember that it was all about where most of the trouble in the world comes from, which is from ignorance and suspicion and people who jump to the wrong conclusions and make what they imagine turn into real trouble. And then he started attacking witch-hunters. I don't know how the Chief had found out about our investigating Jackie's little sister, but he must have heard about it, because why else would he be talking about witch-hunters? He said that witch-hunters, which obviously meant Willie and me, were troublemakers of the worst kind. So it came as a surprise when, just about the time we thought he was going to put us in a cell, he said, "What's it going to be, Andy and Willie? Are you going to be counted with the troublemakers or the peacemakers in the future?"

"We're for the peacemakers," I said, which was true.

"We don't like trouble," said Willie.

"If this is all settled," said Mr. Schmidt, very pleasant, "I'll be going."

"But it's not all settled," said the Chief, very pleasant. "I suppose," he said to Willie and me, "that you've done a lot of talking about the book."

"No," I said. "We talked about it only on the train today coming home from our trip to Chicago. And we wouldn't have talked about it then if we'd known that Edgar Bolger is one of the troublemakers of the world."

"So only a hick cop would believe a crazy kid?" said the Chief to Mr. Schmidt. Then smiling at Willie and me, he added in a grand voice to Mr. Toomey, "Hold that man for further questioning."

Mr. Schmidt looked as if he had been hit on the head. For that matter, so did Willie.

"What?" said Mr. Schmidt. "What? What do you mean? What is this?" Then, pulling himself together, he said, "So they were on the train, and I was on the train. That doesn't prove that I was ever near them before to-night."

"You've got a point," said the Chief, and looking at Willie and me, he said to Mr. Toomey, "Search them."

It was the closest I ever came to giving up being a detective. Nothing was making any sense. Here just as I thought that the Chief was beginning to believe us, he was having us searched as if we were criminals.

"No—er—weapons," said Mr. Toomey, grinning, as he and the Chief looked at the contents of Willie's and my pockets.

"That settles the question," said the Chief. "So you did take the book," he said to Mr. Schmidt.

"Is everybody in this town out of his mind?" said Mr. Schmidt. "What's your evidence? The word of those crazy kids?"

"Yes," said the Chief. "And this," he added, patting the briefcase.

I've told this exactly as it happened. But I bet you don't know yet and couldn't guess in a million years how the Chief deducted that Mr. Schmidt was a thief. Even Willie and I didn't know. But when the Chief said that we should be at home in bed, we didn't stop to ask questions. The way we were feeling, if the Chief said we should be in bed, we were going to take his word for it, even if Howard G. Trillinger was still running around loose. And when my parents took it for granted that we had been at Willie's all evening, we didn't straighten them out, even though it isn't everybody who has just caught a thief from Chicago. We'd had enough danger for one night.

But the next morning Willie and I were feeling peppy again. So after our Sunday School lesson, which was all about forgiveness, we went to the police station to look at Mr. Schmidt behind bars and also to tell him that we didn't have much hard feeling against him for twisting my arm so that it was probably sprained for life and knocking Willie around in such a mean way. We were counting on the Chief's not being on duty since it was Sunday. Even though he'd ended up being friendly to us the night before, we weren't forgetting how unfriendly he'd been at first. So we reconnoitered. We found the outer office empty, but when we peeped through the window of the Chief's office, there he sat drinking coffee with Hubert Welsh's father. However, they were laughing, and since the Chief appeared to be in good spirits, we decided to take a chance and go in. Besides, Hubert's father publishes the Wakanda News, and we figured that there wouldn't be any police brutality with a member of the press present.

When the Chief heard that we'd come to forgive Mr. Schmidt, he said, "Now that's more like it. People like Mr. Schmidt need a lot of forgiving. Unfortunately, you probably won't ever be able to give him the pleasure of forgiving him in person. When I put Mr. Schmidt on the train last night, he wasn't planning to come this way again."

Willie and I were astounded to hear that the Chief had let our public enemy go free. Even if Mr. Bolger didn't prefer charges, we did. After all, Mr. Schmidt had twisted my arm so that it was probably sprained for life and had knocked Willie around in a mean way. We'd thought that he would get at least five years, and we were already counting on visiting the prison regularly in order to forgive him and brighten up his day and rehabilitate him. As Willie said, the Chief's letting him go ruined all our plans for becoming famous forgivers.

However, we were about to discover how fantastically brainy the Chief is, and as Willie says, anybody with such a brain is entitled to one mistake. Finding the Chief so full of peace, we got up the nerve to ask him about the evidence in the briefcase and the weapons which Willie and I didn't have. At first, the Chief, and Mr. Welsh, too, just laughed. In fact, they laughed so much at nothing that Willie said later he thought there was something in that coffee besides coffee. But I don't think so, especially with a member of the press present.

Anyway, finally the Chief said, "See these initials you put on my desk blotter, Willie? Now what do you suppose I saw on Mr. Schmidt's briefcase?"

"My initials?" said Willie in a depressed voice, thinking he was in new trouble.

"Yes. And if you didn't have an ink pad and stamp —weapons, that is—with you, when did the initials get on the briefcase?"

"On the train!" I said. "So Mr. Schmidt wasn't telling the truth when he said he wasn't near us on the train. He must have heard us talking about the book."

"Poor Mr. Schmidt," said Mr. Welsh. Hubert said later that his father has a habit of missing the point like this. I mean, the big point here was the Chief's fantastic brain. Willie and I weren't missing it.

"What an amazing, terrific, fantastic deduction!" said Willie.

"Sherlock Holmes couldn't have done better," I said.

"I have my moments of greatness," said the Chief. "And now," he added, "will you take my word for it that Doctor Truesdale is not wanted by the FBI? His father, by the way, is a cousin of mine, and I assure you that his name is not Trillinger."

I don't know why the Chief hadn't mentioned this before. But I suppose it is embarrassing to have to own up to so many suspicious-looking relatives. At any rate, we told him that we certainly did take his word for it and promised that in the future we'd leave it to him to catch the men on the Wanted posters.

But the best part came later. The Chief said that since Willie was so bent on stamping everything in sight, he might as well leave behind him something worth reading. So the Chief had stamps made for us both in fancy letters saying, "Blessed Are the Peacemakers." And best of all—although it did have some unpleasant end results when our fathers saw it—there was an article in the Monday *Wakanda News* about Mr. Schmidt and Caesar and Willie and me. It called Willie and me "intrepid," which means "fearless," "bold," "dauntless," "valiant," "brave," "courageous," because Willie and I looked it up in the dictionary. Just as Jackie's little sister had predicted, we got our names in the paper for solving a big case. And since it was a good prediction, we'd furnished absolute proof that Jackie's little sister wasn't a witch. All the kids, except Ronald, who was furious at all the publicity we were getting, said that we were probably the greatest detectives in the world for our weight.

I might add that it was lucky for Jackie's little sister that her good prediction came true right at this point, because the one thing the Chief really insisted on before we left the station that Saturday night was that we give up witch-hunting. He never mentioned Jackie's little sister by name and so we didn't either, but it was plain to see that our other case was on his mind. So we promised to give up witch-hunting forever, though it did seem tough on Jackie's little sister that she wouldn't have us to protect her from Ronald's accusations. Luckily, the news article took care of everything.

We told Archie and Freddie and all the other kids what the Chief had said about suspicion and ignorance and accusations. So everybody got mad at Ronald for making suspicious, ignorant accusations against Jackie's little sister. William Henry said that Ronald was an old witch. And everybody agreed that it's the best explanation anyone ever thought of to account for Ronald Pruitt. At least, as Willie pointed out, a person with so much information about witches must have known a lot of them personally.

Chapter XXIV
A BLOODCURDLING PERFORMANCE

After Willie and I caught the big thief from Chicago, Mr. Schmidt, and got our names in the Wakanda newspaper, we didn't do any detecting for quite a while. You might think that when we'd just succeeded in protecting the town from a public enemy and getting a little fame, our fathers would be pleased. But the way my father carried on, you couldn't tell whether the public enemy was Mr. Schmidt or me. I got a first-degree paddling. And my father told me that if I got any more famous for my detective work, I'd also be famous for not being able to sit down. Willie got a paddling, too, and as he said, getting spanked for catching a crook can be discouraging. So we decided to give up the detective business until our fathers had simmered down.

Besides, Miss Easter was sold on a lot of dumb homework for everybody in the fifth grade, and she started piling this dumb homework on us to the point where we didn't have a chance to concentrate on anything important anyway, except fifth grade basketball practice and an occasional look at television every night. Then Melville Miller disappeared, and Willie and I were back in business again.

It all started with the play about the birth of Christ which our class wrote and acted out for the first grade students. Miss Easter had told us that she'd learned in an education course how educational it was for young people to write and act out their own version of great events, and so at first she said that she would leave the whole performance up to us. But then she kept asking to see the script, which Betsy Miller, who is the best speller in class, was writing at the dictation of anyone who had a good version we all approved of. And every time Miss Easter read the script she practically ruined the play cutting out our best ideas. For example, at the beginning of the play, to show how revolting Herod was, we had this scene where he ate worms. He was really going to eat spaghetti, but the announcer who explained the scenes to the first grade audience was going to tell them it was worms. But Miss Easter said that we were getting too far away from fact, and she made us cut the scene out. Her standing up for Herod like that made you wonder whose side she was on. Anyway, she kept cutting out all the best scenes, and finally she went too far. Willie had suggested that we have the angels sing "Way down upon the Swanee River" when Mary and Joseph were wandering in the desert. It was perfect to describe someone away from home. But Miss Easter couldn't see it that way. So all the class got disgusted because she'd said it was to be our version and here she was welshing on the deal and insisting on her version.

At this point when it looked as if we wouldn't be putting on a play after all, Mr. Barrie said to Miss Easter, "Surely you aren't letting your faith in education courses weaken." For some reason this annoyed Miss Easter. And the outcome was that she told us to go ahead with our own version. Without her interfering and spoiling everything, we ended up with a really interesting play.

We were afraid, though, at first that it would be a failure because of Miss Easter's bad casting. For instance, she cast Willie as Joseph, who had the least to do of anybody in the play. All Joseph did was just stand around. And when she cast Betsy Miller as Mary, Betsy kept thinking that just because Joseph was her husband in the play, she could tell Willie what to do. Willie said he didn't know what got into Miss Easter making him be Joseph.

She cast Freddie Clark as an angel, which is about as dumb casting as you can get, because the angels had to wear big wings and Freddie always has too much on his mind to pay attention to what he's wearing. Freddie is the type of person who is as likely to wear his wings in front as behind. Freddie should have been a wise man. And she cast Morris Somers as an angel, too, which was especially dumb, because the angels had to sing all the time, and as Willie pointed out, Homer XI, who had the worst voice of any frog Willie ever had, sounded better than Morris Somers. Morris ruins every song he's in. But the worst casting of all was letting Ronald Pruitt be the main Roman soldier who got to carry a spear and shove everybody around. I can beat Ronald Pruitt in a fight any day. Ronald should have been the social chairman, who got beheaded in the first scene, or an angel on the back row.

However, Miss Easter did one good piece of casting in spite of herself. At first, everybody was disgusted when she picked Jackie Carr to play Herod. Everybody knows that Herod was the wide-awake type. And the kind of person Jackie is, if he's playing right field and somebody hits a high fly in his direction, there is Jackie flat on his back asleep. But as it turned out, it's a good thing Miss Easter wouldn't listen to our criticism about Jackie's not being right for the part of Herod, because Jackie turned out to be a natural born actor. When he got that crown on and the black whiskers which Freddie brought for him to wear and the dark glasses, which celebrities like Herod always wear, something just seemed to come over Jackie. He looked revolting, and he acted revolting. And in practice he was always having brainstorms and adding good, mean things to his part. For example, once in practice when Ronald, who was standing near the throne, bent over to tie his shoelaces, Jackie said, "No one ties his shoes in the presence of the king," and he put his foot on Ronald's rear end and shoved him clear across the stage on his face. Ronald was burned up, since it wasn't in the script. But everybody thought it was such a good touch that we wrote it in. Jackie kept thinking of touches like this all the time, mostly in regard to Ronald, to show that Herod was so mean, he was mean even to his own gang. The part of the main Roman soldier changed quite a lot after Ronald Pruitt got it.

A thing about Jackie that I should mention is that he was so carried away by his part in the play that he started acting like Herod all the time. He snarled around from morning to night. Once when we were leaving school, Willie accidentally stepped on Jackie's toe, and Jackie got so outraged at Willie for stepping on a king's toe that he pushed Willie into a big pile of snow at the edge of the walk. But when he was Jackie Carr, he was one of our best friends and wouldn't hurt anybody for anything. So for the good of the play we decided to put up with the way he was acting until after the performance was over.

Miss Easter wanted us to use a doll for Jesus. But we wanted Jesus to be alive. So Betsy Miller suggested her little brother Melville. She said that Melville, who was three, had led a very protected life and would be perfect for the part. It turned out she was right. When the teachers first saw Melville, they all said, "Oh, what a beautiful child!" But the important thing was that Melville is a good kid. He was a perfect choice.

With Jackie being great and Melville being perfect, the bad casting was less noticeable. Besides, Archie Monroe and I were two of the wise men, which was good casting. You can't put anything over on Archie and me. And since Hubert Welsh puts out a newspaper in real life, he was good as the voice that yelled every once in a while, "Beware, Herod. Beware. Beware. Beware."

Of course, some of the kids never did stop griping about the casting. Agatha Crawley was furious because she said that she would have been an ideal Mary. And she was jealous because her little brother Edsel wasn't chosen instead of Melville. It's a good thing he wasn't. Edsel Crawley is a holy terror. And the only thing you could criticize Melville for was that he hid from people. Betsy brought him to practice three times, and every time he hid in the closet and under desks, and we were always having to hunt for him. Once we got him on the hay, though, he was OK. And all the time he was likable. I wouldn't mind having a little brother like Melville myself.

We were to give the first performance of the play in

the morning before Christmas vacation for the first grade and the second performance in the afternoon for the second and third grades. As it turned out, the first performance was the only one we gave, but it was really great. Jackie Carr was terrific.

The opening scene showed how mean Herod was and why he decided to kill all the babies. To begin with, he got bored because the news on television was always the same. He was listening to the news, and he got more and more bored and mad, and finally when the announcer said that the United States was still standing firm on Cuba, which still wouldn't let anybody inspect its bases, he tore up the television set. You should have seen Herod rip up the box that stood for the television cabinet. Then Herod sent for the ice cream man so that he could eat and enjoy himself. The ice cream man named fifteen flavors, but Herod had tried them all before. So when the ice cream man said there wasn't any new kind of ice cream, Herod had him beheaded. Then he sent for the dancing girls. But they didn't know any new dances except the twist, and Herod had done the twist. So he had them all beheaded. Then he sent for his social chairman to see whether anything new was lined up for that week. The social chairman said that Herod was to take a ride on an elephant and shoot a tiger, but Herod had already done these things. So he had the social chairman beheaded. Then Herod sat on his throne and thought and thought and thought about something new to do to have some fun. And finally he jumped up and said, "I've got it. I'll kill all the babies."

It was a great scene. And Jackie got better and better as the play continued. All along he kept thinking up new touches. For instance, when Agatha Crawley tried to steal a scene from him by crying so loud over her baby being killed, Jackie had her beheaded. This wasn't in the script, and Agatha was stunned when the soldiers dragged her off the stage, which made the whole thing very realistic. Besides, it was the perfect way to take care of Agatha Crawley. And at the end of the play, after Jesus was born and the angels had sung "Silent Night," Jackie was terrific in the scene where Herod was shown getting the news from the detective. As the curtains came together, Herod was yelling, "I'll get him yet. I'll get him yet."

It was a very successful play. After the performance was over, Nicholas Parsons said to Willie, "Hello, Joseph," which shows the impression the play had made on Nicholas. You may think that Nicholas, who was a year younger than the first graders and only got to visit school and see the play because his mother was the first grade teacher, was carried away by the performance because of his youth. But you should have seen a bunch of the first grade kids scatter and run when Jackie Carr passed by in his whiskers. Even Mr. Barrie said that the play shook him up as few plays ever had. And it was easy to see that it shook up Miss Easter. I guess Jackie's bloodcurdling performance showed her that she shouldn't let her faith in education courses weaken.

Chapter XXV
A STRANGE DISAPPEARANCE

After the play was over, we went back to our room to have our Christmas exchange. Freddie had drawn my name, and he gave me a swell gold whistle. We were supposed to spend only a quarter on our gifts, but Freddie said that actually the whistle cost him thirty-seven cents with tax. Freddie said he wouldn't have spent that much on everybody. Willie had had the bad luck to draw Ronald Pruitt's name. He had tried to get Miss Easter to let him trade with somebody, but Miss Easter yelled at him for about a half hour about being kind and loving at Christmas time. So when Willie saw that he was stuck with giving Ronald something, he got this idea. He bought Ronald a bottle of iodine, because if you drink it, it's poison. We all knew about it before the exchange, because just after the play while we were still in the room where the performance was given, Willie had told us he was giving Ronald something to murder himself with and start the new year right.

After the exchange, we had lunch and then we started getting ready to give the play for the third grade, though Miss Easter said she didn't think she could live through another performance, which shows how blood-curdling Jackie was. But we never gave the play again because Melville Miller had disappeared. Betsy had left Melville in the first grade room to play in the sandbox and eat lunch with the little kids. And the first grade teacher thought Betsy had come and taken Melville away. Besides, since vacation was coming, there was a lot of excitement, and everyone was running around out of place. So Melville disappeared without anybody's noticing it.

At first, no one was especially upset. People just thought that Melville had gone into hiding again. So Miss Easter gave us a geography assignment and started looking for Melville in closets and under desks all over the building. But she and all the other teachers looked and looked, and Melville was still missing. Then Betsy Miller began to get hysterical.

"My mother will never forgive me," Betsy said, "if Melville gets lost for good, especially right before Christmas."

"We'll find Melville soon," said Miss Easter. But she was beginning to look worried.

Nobody had had the sense to consult Willie and me, even though we were the only detectives in school, but naturally we were giving the case our attention instead of working on the geography assignment. It was obviously a lot more important to find out where Melville was than where the capitals of the world were, which was already known anyway. The thing that struck Willie and me as peculiar was that Melville, who had never been a good hider, could stay out of sight so long. So finally Willie and I went out into the hall and suggested to Miss Easter that Melville might have crawled into a locker that accidentally got locked. Miss Easter told us to tend to our geography lesson, but later Willie and I heard all the lockers banging all over the building. There must have been about a million and Melville wasn't in any of them, which may have been the reason Miss Easter wouldn't listen when Willie and I went out into the hall again and told her we had decided that Melville had obviously been kidnapped.

"And the only people with a reason to kidnap Melville," said Willie, "are obviously Agatha Crawley so that Edsel can be in the play, or Ronald Pruitt on general principles."

Well, Willie and I found out right away that there was no point in trying to cooperate with Miss Easter.

"I thought I told you," she said, "to get to work on your geography assignment and leave the problem of finding Melville to me."

It was obvious that we would have to investigate Agatha and Ronald on our own. So when we went back to class, we told them that we'd reported them as being under suspicion for kidnapping. Everybody, except Jackie Carr, who was asleep, got worked up against Agatha and Ronald for kidnapping Melville. You never saw anybody as mad as Agatha Crawley.

"You are mean, bad boys," she said to Willie and me. "I wouldn't even think of being a kidnapper."

She and Ronald both went out into the hall to look for Miss Easter to tell her that they weren't kidnappers, and the whole class got pretty noisy, what with everyone criticizing Agatha or Ronald, and Betsy Miller having hysterics over Melville being kidnapped just before Christmas. So then Miss Easter came in as mad as all get out. She quieted everybody down and told Willie and me that if we caused any more trouble, we'd have to stay in after school. That's the way Miss Easter shows the Christmas spirit.

After she left, Ronald said, "Andy and Willie couldn't detect their way out of a swimming pool." Some of the kids laughed. "They couldn't detect a whale in a bathtub," said Ronald. "If they're detectives, I'm Buffalo Bill."

We knew that Ronald was trying to get us to do something so that we'd have to stay in after school, and so we ignored him.

But then he said, "Willie is an Indian giver."

"I am not," said Willie. "You'd better be careful."

"You are," said Ronald. "I left the iodine on top of my desk when I went to lunch, and when I came back, it was gone. So it's obvious that you took it back. You're an Indian giver."

Well, as Willie was getting ready to go for Ronald and Ronald was getting ready to run for Miss Easter, suddenly I made this terrible deduction. I grabbed Willie, who sits in front of me, and shoved him back into his seat.

"Let go," said Willie. "Nobody calls me an Indian giver and gets away with it."

"If the poison disappeared when Melville disappeared, maybe someone murdered Melville," I said to Willie in a whisper.

Willie forgot all about being called an Indian giver.

"Who would murder a little kid?" said Willie. But he knew what I was thinking. We hated to think it out loud. We both looked at Jackie Carr, who was still asleep.

"What'll we do?" said Willie. "Jackie is a friend of ours. He wouldn't hurt anybody."

"Well, Herod isn't," I said. "And Herod would."

It was a bloodcurdling thought. But everybody knew how Jackie had been carried away by the part of Herod.

"Somebody's got to tell Miss Easter," I said.

"I'm not going to," said Willie. "She won't listen to reason, anyway. And I don't want to stay in after school."

"What we'll have to do is prove it and then tell her," I said. "Maybe they'll let Jackie off easy since Herod did it."

So Willie and I went to Jackie's seat and got on both sides of him and shook him. Jackie woke up as Herod.

"Take your hands off me," he said in this revolting voice. "I'll get you for this."

"What did you do with the body?" I said.

Herod turned into Jackie. "What body?" he said.

"Melville Miller. What did you do with him?"

Jackie looked surprised. "I never did nothing with nobody," he said.

Willie and I were trying to be quiet, but all the kids were trying to hear. And Hubert Welsh, who sits in front of Jackie, had guessed what was going on. Since Hubert puts out a newspaper, he always thinks that if there's any news, it is his duty to inform the public.

"Herod got Melville," he told the rest of the class.

You never heard such a racket. Agatha said that Jackie was a mean, bad boy, and Betsy began to have hysterics over Herod's getting Melville right before Christmas. Jackie kept saying that he wouldn't hurt Melville or anybody else, but after his performance, everybody knew that Herod would. In the midst of all this, in came Miss Easter, looking quite hot. Ronald, as it turned out, had gone to get her as soon as Willie and I started to question Jackie. And the outcome of it all was that Miss Easter said that Melville had not been kidnapped or killed, that Jackie was not to blame for Melville's disappearance, and that Willie and I were to stay in after school for causing another disturbance.

"How does she know any of that except about our staying in?" said Willie, after Miss Easter had got everyone back to work and had left the room again.

It was disgusting, but there was nothing we could think of to do. We knew from experience that no one can reason with Miss Easter. The period passed, and the next period, too, and Melville was still missing. Miss Easter came back, looking very nervous, and gave us an arithmetic assignment in subtraction. Melville's mother came to school to yell all over the building for Melville. Betsy was taken out of class to answer questions, and we could hear her having hysterics in the hall about Melville and Christmas. All the kids began to get jumpy. Even Mr. Barrie, who is usually calm, looked worried. He had heard what Willie and I had said about Agatha, Ronald, and Jackie, and unlike most teachers I could name, Mr. Barrie always pays attention to what kids say. So he came into our classroom to ask questions. But Jackie swore that he'd never seen Melville after the performance. He sounded so innocent that even Willie and I were almost convinced. Up to then, with the poison missing, we'd been sure that the case was solved and Herod was the villain. If Jackie was innocent, it was good news. But, on the other hand, it looked as if the only explanation left was that Melville had dropped into a hole and the ground had closed up, which was almost as bloodcurdling as suspecting Herod.

Chapter XXVI
A GOOD DEAL OF GLORY

It was at this point in the case, just after Mr. Barrie left the room, that I discovered that my gold whistle was missing. I distinctly remembered leaving it on my desk when I went to lunch, but nevertheless I looked inside my desk and in all of my pockets to be sure. It was gone. I asked whether anybody in the class had seen it, but nobody had.

"Now the great detective is going to announce that Melville stole his whistle and my poison and skipped town," said Ronald.

Of course, this was one of Ronald's typical wise-cracks. Obviously, Melville's legs were so little that it would take him a month to skip town, and, besides, his coat was still hanging in the closet. But it did occur to me that if Melville and the whistle and the poison were connected, maybe Willie and I could clear Jackie and solve the case all over again. Herod might have taken the poison, but he wouldn't have any reason that I could think of to take the whistle.

There was no point in working on subtraction problems at a time like this. I poked Willie in the back.

"Willie," I said, "there's got to be a connection between all these disappearances. Let's start over and give this a good thinking and eliminate suspects the way detectives do in stories."

"I'm ready," said Willie.

"First, Melville is too little to hide successfully this long. So we can eliminate Melville. Does that make sense?"

"It makes sense to me," said Willie.

"Second, Herod is the only person who would kill Melville. But neither Jackie nor Herod would take my whistle. Besides, I have a feeling now that Herod didn't do it. Also, I want Jackie to be innocent. So we can eliminate both Herod and Jackie. Does that make sense?"

"It certainly does," said Willie.

"All right," I said, "therefore, Melville was kidnapped."

"That makes sense," said Willie.

"Now the only persons we've thought of who would kidnap Melville are Agatha and Ronald. But, third, we can eliminate Agatha because she suspected Herod. And, fourth, we can eliminate Ronald because he wouldn't steal his own poison. Does that make sense?"

"No," said Willie. "Maybe Agatha just pretended to suspect Herod. And maybe Ronald just said his poison was stolen so that he could lay a false trail. I don't see what the poison has to do with a kidnapper anyway."

"Neither do I. But we can still eliminate people if it makes sense. And my whistle is gone. Why would Agatha or Ronald steal my whistle? That is, if there is a connection between all these missing objects."

"Maybe they offered Melville the whistle to lure him away."

"But when would they do it? My whistle was stolen during lunch. They were eating when we were," I said.

"You're right," said Willie. "We'll eliminate them because it makes sense. We're getting good at this, aren't we? Now we've got everybody eliminated, and we are really getting somewhere. So who did it?"

"Somebody besides Agatha and Ronald who had a reason for kidnapping Melville," I said, "and for taking a whistle and some poison."

"This is what I call progress," said Willie.

But we racked our brains, and we couldn't figure out anybody else who'd have a reason for kidnapping Melville.

"I have an idea," said Willie finally. "Maybe Melville thought that he was the part he played the way Jackie thought that he was Herod."

"What's that got to do with somebody's kidnapping him?" I said.

But as I asked the question, I knew the answer. It was so obvious that I don't know why we hadn't thought of it before.

"Willie," I said, pounding him on the back, "we've got it."

"What did I say?" said Willie.

"We've been trying to figure out who kidnapped Melville because he was Melville," I said. "And we've eliminated everybody. So he must have been kidnapped because somebody thought that he was the part he played. Does that make sense?"

"It's the most sense I ever heard," said Willie. "Now all we have to do is to find out who could be that mixed up."

"I know that," I said.

As a result of my brainstorm I could hardly sit still in my seat, and all the people in class knew that an important deduction was taking place, but they didn't know what deduction because Willie and I had been whispering. Ronald, who sits across from me, was trying to eavesdrop, and so I whispered the name of the kidnapper in Willie's ear.

"Are you sure?" said Willie.

"Positive," I said.

"How do you know?" said Willie. "Why would he do such a thing? What's his connection with the whistle and the poison?"

"I don't know everything," I said. "This case is filled with mystery. But I do know that he's the kidnapper. And he lives next door to the school, which explains why Melville's coat is still in the closet and why nobody can find Melville here."

"You're right," said Willie, forgetting to whisper in his excitement. "He's got to be the kidnapper."

"They've solved the case," Hubert Welsh told the class.

Well, you've never heard such a racket. Everybody started talking and asking questions except Ronald Pruitt, who got up to go tell Miss Easter that we were causing a disturbance. Willie and I grabbed Ronald.

"Hang on to Ronald," I told Hubert and Freddie Clark and Archie Monroe. "Don't let him go for Miss Easter. We've got to leave on business, and we'll try to get back before Miss Easter finds out we've left."

We peeped out into the hall. It was empty. Everyone was off hunting.

"We're really going to be in trouble if we're wrong," said Willie, as we went through the hall and down the steps and out through a side door. "Maybe we'll be expelled."

"We can't be wrong," I said.

And we weren't. Nicholas Parsons answered our knock at the house next door.

"Hello, Joseph," he said to Willie.

"We've come for Jesus," I said.

"All right," said Nicholas. "But you won't let Herod get him, will you? Everybody went away and left him all by himself. And Herod said that he was going to get him. I've been hiding him from Herod."

"We won't let Herod get him," said Willie.

So Nicholas took us upstairs, and there was Melville sound asleep.

"My grandmama is taking a nap, too," said Nicholas. "Everybody here is taking a nap except me. I'm protecting Jesus. Even my grandmama doesn't know that Jesus is here. I protected him pretty well, didn't I?"

We told him he had, and we took Melville back to school after promising Nicholas at least a dozen times that we wouldn't leave Melville unprotected again and that we wouldn't let Herod get him.

There was a big commotion when Willie and I returned with Melville. Melville's mother kept hugging us along with Melville. Betsy said that we were heroes. Agatha said that we were good, nice boys. All the kids, except Ronald, said that we were the most outstanding detectives they had ever even heard of. Mr. Barrie shook hands with us, and after he told Miss Easter that our elimination of the suspects was a remarkable exercise in subtraction, she said that under the circumstances she would excuse us for not working on her assignment and we wouldn't have to stay in after school. Ronald, who was burned up as usual to see Willie and me admired, told everybody later that his brother Bertie said it took one to detect one. But, as Willie said, there are worse things than being compared to someone who wanted to keep Jesus alive.

There was a discovery and an unusual result from all this which Willie and I didn't ever tell anybody except Freddie Clark and Mr. McCotter. The discovery was the gold whistle and the iodine on the table beside the bed where Melville was sleeping. It seems that after the play when Willie was making that wisecrack about the iodine gift for Ronald to murder himself with and when Freddie was telling about the gold whistle he was giving me, Nicholas was standing there listening. Nicholas said that he knew we'd be glad he took the gifts since they were gifts for Jesus. He said he couldn't find any frankincense, but he knew that two of the things people gave to Jesus were gold and murder. Little kids like Nicholas get everything all mixed up, but as Willie admitted, this mistake was partly Willie's own fault. So I let Melville keep the gold whistle, since he was so crazy about it. But Willie and I threw the iodine away on the walk back to school. Somehow, after what Nicholas had said, the iodine gift didn't seem so funny. And the unusual result was that Willie sent Ronald a good bouncing ball in the mail. He sent it anonymous, for fear Ronald would get the idea that Willie had gone soft.

And we didn't squeal on Nicholas for taking the gifts. For one thing, we didn't want Ronald accusing him of theft, and for another thing, we somehow didn't want anybody making fun of him. It seemed to us that since Nicholas had tried to protect Jesus, the least we could do was to try to protect Nicholas.

Mr. McCotter says that he thinks all of our decisions were the right ones. And he says that of all our cases this one probably got us the most glory in the long run.

Chapter XXVII
A MATTER OF NATIONAL SECURITY

Willie and Archie Monroe spent quite a lot of last Christmas vacation looking up. They had both got new sleds for Christmas. But all through vacation time there was no snow. We were gloomy about it until we talked to Mr. McCotter.

"If there's one thing you can count on in this life, it's change," said Mr. McCotter, who always spends his winters sitting on a bench in Miller's Hardware Store criticizing the government in Washington and who had taken advantage of the weather to move back to the bench in front of the post office where he could keep an eye on Main

Street. "All you have to do is be philosophic and hope for the best."

So Willie and Archie and I got philosophic, and sure enough, about three days after school reopened, it snowed so hard and the snow drifted so high that the school busses couldn't get into town from the country and school was closed for a week, which shows that philosophy really pays off. January and most of February were cold and snowy and great. Big Walnut Creek froze as hard as stone, and one Saturday night when the high school boys built big bonfires all along the creek, my father took Willie, Freddie, Archie, and me ice-skating. It was great. As Willie said, we'd hoped for the best and we got it.

What with the snow and the ice, Willie and I almost forgot about our detective career. Then late in February something happened which led to one of the most unsolved mysteries in Wakanda's history, since I was the only one who solved it. It all began one day in class when Agatha Crawley announced that she was going to run for President when she grew up. Everybody in the fifth grade with any sense got gloomy at the prospect. Agatha is the type that if she set her mind on being President, she just might make it, and nothing could be worse for the United States. All of us with any sense said so right away.

"If Agatha becomes President, I may move to Canada," said Morris Somers.

"In my opinion, the United States can get along without Morris," said Agatha in her most superior tone.

This gives some idea about Agatha Crawley. Everybody knows that Morris is going to send a lot of people into outer space some day. Everybody with sense knows that the United States needs scientists like Morris Somers.

"Actually, if more men would move away, there would be less danger of wars," Agatha added, "since men are the ones who start wars."

"There isn't anybody more warlike than Agatha Crawley," said Willie.

"If she starts bossing the United States," said Hubert Welsh, "we're done for."

"It gives me the heebie-jeebies to even think of it," said Morris. "Why doesn't Agatha stick to girls' business?"

"You don't need to say any more," said Agatha. "I have now definitely made up my mind to be President."

As if this weren't bad enough, Miss Easter, who at first had just tried to keep everybody calm, came in on Agatha's side. "What do you mean by girls' business?" she said to Morris. "Perhaps you are being influenced by prejudice."

"If being against Agatha is being prejudiced, I am for sure," said Morris.

"Now, Morris," said Miss Easter, "as a responsible citizen, you must be guided by reason, and it isn't reasonable to be against a woman for President just because she is a woman."

"Why not?" said Hubert.

Then he was sorry he asked, because Miss Easter told him for so long that we all got to feeling worn out. I mean, obviously we all believe in reason, and we all believe in paying attention to a candidate's principles and platform. But what has all this to do with the fact that a bossy girl like Agatha Crawley just isn't cut out to be President? However, the tireder we got, the peppier Miss Easter got. And when she saw that no matter what she said, none of us with any sense would give an inch on Agatha for President, she developed this idea of a project to teach us to be reasonable voters. She said that we'd elect a class president, but not just by nominating some people on the spur of the moment and voting immediately. This election was going to be long drawn out and complicated, so that we could learn to be reasonable. There would be nominating speeches, and the candidates would speak on their plans for improving the fifth grade in particular and the school in general. This way we'd learn to take a candidate's principles and platforms into consideration and be responsible citizens.

Since it was late in February, whoever was elected wouldn't have the title long. Besides, according to what Miss Easter was planning, the president was going to have to give a lot of time to improving the school with the baseball season coming up. So none of the boys was interested in Miss Easter's project. But it sometimes happened that the less interested we were, the more interested Miss Easter was. She and the class were hardly ever interested at the same time. When we started to get enthusiastic, she usually acted as if she wanted to forget the whole thing. And that's what happened during this project.

She started out telling us about laws, political parties, what went on during primary elections and conventions, et cetera. We were supposed to be thinking, choosing candidates, and writing nominating speeches, but with the baseball season coming up, so far as I knew nobody was thinking, et cetera. After all, it wasn't as if we were picking the President of the United States, even if Miss Easter did seem to have the two elections mixed up. But one morning when we were lined up on our way to the drinking fountain, we heard something which changed our whole attitude.

"Agatha," said Betsy Miller in this loud voice, "are you going to run for the presidency?"

"Positively not," said Agatha. "I wouldn't even think of it."

"I heard that you were planning to run," said Barbie Reagan.

"You have been misinformed," said Agatha. "I absolutely refuse to run under any circumstances."

"If you were drafted, would you accept the draft?" said Betsy.

"I'll always be ready to do my duty and serve the people," said Agatha, "but I don't foresee a draft."

This whole dumb conversation was carried on in the loud voices girls use when they have a purpose.

"What was that all about?" said Willie.

"Agatha is going to run for president," said Hubert, who is up on politics because he is a newspaperman. "You talk that way so that you can surprise everybody."

Sure enough, during recess we found out that Betsy was going to nominate Agatha, who was already writing her acceptance speech and organizing the girls into a party. They called it the People's Party.

Morris was horrified by the news. "If Agatha wins," he said, "and gets a taste of power, she'll probably keep on until she's President of the United States and is ruining everything. We ought to stop her before she gets going."

"I think Morris is right," said Hubert. "This whole business is turning into a matter of national security."

None of us wanted to run against Agatha with the baseball season coming up, but with the United States in danger, it was obvious that one of us had to be a candidate. So we drew straws, and Hubert got the nomination. Actually, since Hubert knows a lot of political terms, it seemed then like a lucky draw. I don't know what would have happened if Willie had drawn the short stick. He had said that considering Agatha's personality, a lot of things could happen to her before she got old enough to be President, and he wanted to be philosophic and hope for the best while taking advantage of the baseball season. In fact, he finally agreed to draw straws only because Hubert insisted that it was a matter of responsible citizenship. And, as everybody knows, if there's anything going on, Willie is responsible.

We got busy organizing against Agatha and the People's Party right away. The first thing we did was to name us the Party of the Other People. Our biggest problem was that there were fourteen girls in the class and only eleven boys, and Hubert said that since Agatha had probably organized all the girls into joining the People's Party, what we had to do was to break the vote of the solid girls, which Hubert explained was the political way of putting it. And Hubert figured that one way to do this was to have Freddie give the speech nominating Hubert because one of the solidest girls in class was Edna Marie Jennings, who weighs at least eighty-five pounds and likes Freddie. But Freddie didn't want to stand where he'd have to see Edna Marie, who has an obnoxious habit of beaming at Freddie.

"Besides," said Freddie, "I don't have time to write a speech."

"I'll write the speech," said Hubert. "And, besides, this is a matter of responsible citizenship."

So Freddie finally agreed. But then Hubert went so far as to ask Freddie to show his patriotism by speaking in a friendly way to Edna Marie. Freddie put his foot down.

"I'll give the speech," he told Hubert, "since it's a matter of national security for you to get the vote of the solid girls, but it's against my principles to speak to them in a social way."

"Even Nathan Hale wouldn't be that patriotic," Freddie told me later. "I think that politics is making Hubert unreasonable."

Chapter XXVIII
CANDIDATES AND CAMPAIGNS

I won't go into the details of Betsy's and Freddie's nominating speeches or the first speeches made by Agatha and Hubert, which all took place in the next few days. I will say that Freddie had a lot of trouble reading Hubert's handwriting. For example, he bogged down three times on the last line.

"And so I nominate Hubert T. Welsh, a——" Freddie said and then stopped because he couldn't make out the word.

"Brilliant," whispered Hubert from the middle of the room.

"A brilliant newspaperman, a——" Freddie stopped again and raised his eyebrows at Hubert.

"Prominent," whispered Hubert.

"A brilliant newspaperman, a prominent Boy Scout, and a——"

"Distinguished," hissed Hubert.

"And a distinguished local public servant," said Freddie.

Hubert's having to interpret like this slightly spoiled the effect. But Edna Marie said that Freddie had given a divine speech. So we thought that we had got at least one of the girls' votes already.

But we hadn't counted on what Ronald Pruitt might do. You'd think that even Ronald would draw the line at joining the girls, but when he heard that Hubert had appointed me his campaign manager, Ronald offered his services as campaign manager to Agatha. So even if we did have Edna Marie's vote, Agatha had Ronald's, and the estimated count was back to fourteen to eleven. Also, we knew that now we'd be up against an underhanded campaign.

To make matters worse, the harder the Other People's Party worked to save the country, the more it looked as if Miss Easter was against us, too. For instance, Hubert used his newspaper equipment to make a couple of dozen campaign posters, and the next morning I had just finished fastening them with Scotch tape all over the blackboards and walls when Miss Easter came in and made me take them all down. She finally let me put one poster on the bulletin board, but it was the one Hubert made when he was running out of pep. All it said was "Vote for H. T. Welsh and sane government." Miss Easter hated all the posters. But, as Hubert said, when you are up against an authority who is guided by prejudice, you do the best you can. So during study period, we managed to circulate several of the posters, and they made quite an impression, especially the one that said, "Are you a nut? Then vote for Agatha Crawley." Agatha was furious. And Ronald was jealous because he hadn't thought of posters. So during recess Ronald resorted to a dirty campaign.

What happened first was that Willie and Archie got into a fight because Archie, who had always played shortstop, announced that this year he was going to try for first base. Willie has always considered first base his own private property. But Archie is smart and quick, and if there was anyone who could take first base away from Willie, it was Archie. So Willie was scared, and he insisted that Archie's best position was shortstop and there was no point in Archie's even trying for first base because he, Willie, could run rings around Archie as first baseman. So Archie said he could run rings around Willie in any position. So one word led to another and finally Willie and Archie got into a fight. And after Miss Easter got them pulled apart and while we were lining up to march back to class, Ronald started whispering to Agatha. He whispered and whispered. Then Agatha and Betsy began to whisper and look at Willie.

"What's all the whispering about?" said Willie.

"You're a racist," said Ronald.

Ronald is always looking for words in the dictionary

to call Willie and me, and we never know until we check the dictionary exactly how mad to get. But Willie knew whatever it was, it was an insult.

"Who's a racist? You're a racist," he said to Ronald. "You're the biggest racist that ever lived. What's a racist?" he said to me.

"A racist is against colored people," said Agatha. "Ronald says that everybody in the Other People's Party is a racist," she told the girls.

This shows what you're up against with a creep like Ronald Pruitt around. Archie was in the Other People's Party. Besides, he was Willie's second best friend after me, though right at this point Archie and Willie were enemies because of first base.

"I'm against Archie," said Willie. "That doesn't mean I'm against colored people. You're the whitest-skinned person anywhere around," he said to Ronald, "and I'm against you all the time. What does that make me?"

"You're a racist," said Ronald.

Ronald thought that he was safe because Miss Easter was just inside the building, waiting to march us in. But since Willie was already in trouble because of his fight with Archie, he probably figured that he didn't have much to lose. And before anybody knew what he was doing, he punched Ronald. I didn't know that Willie had such a powerful punch in him, and Archie and Freddie said later that it was the most interesting punch they'd ever seen because Willie punched Ronald so hard that he also knocked down Agatha and Betsy, who were standing behind Ronald.

So then Miss Easter marched Willie to the principal's

155

office where he got a paddling for fighting twice in one recess and not telling why. Willie said the next day that every time he looked at Ronald's black eye, it seemed worth the trouble. But Hubert was afraid that Ronald would be able to use his black eye against the Other People's Party, and Hubert was right. The girls all said that Willie should have hit Ronald a little easier, and Ronald capitalized on their sympathetic feeling by putting a lot of untrue ideas into their heads. For example, Agatha said that it was obvious that her worthy opponent Hubert, being a friend of Willie's, was in favor of the use of violence.

"I'm not in favor of violence," said Hubert.

"You've got a funny way of showing it," said Agatha. "Did *you* get the black eye defending Archie? No. It was Ronald, a member of the People's Party."

"I don't understand this argument," said Hubert.

"You wouldn't," said Agatha, "because you and the Other People's Party are against people's rights. The People's Party," said Agatha in her superior way, "is supporting Archie for first baseman."

"Who needs it?" said Archie. "And Ronald was not defending me. He was picking a fight with Willie."

Ronald and Agatha wouldn't have got anywhere with their untrue claims if Hubert had just left it up to Archie. But as Freddie had said, politics was doing something to Hubert's reason.

"Why don't you show that our party is for people's rights," he said to Willie, "and let Archie be first baseman?"

"What's your trouble? What do you mean?" said Willie. "I'm people."

"Yes, what do you mean?" said Archie. "I'll win

the position for myself because I'll make a better first base-man than Willie ever was."

So Archie and Willie got into another fight, and they both got a paddling. And all the girls acted more superior than ever. They said that it was obvious that the Other People's Party stood for war and violence. And it looked as if Hubert not only wasn't going to get any of the girls' votes but wasn't even going to get Willie's and Archie's, since they both said he must be losing his mind. Hubert figured that evening that the vote would be fourteen to nine, with Willie and Archie abstaining.

"I don't care much for politics," said Hubert. "Here I'm trying to save the country, and I'm losing my best friends."

I felt sorry for Hubert, even if Freddie, Archie, and Willie were right about his turning unreasonable. The next morning Ronald put up a lot of posters praising Agatha for peace and justice and attacking Hubert for violence and injustice, and all the girls started acting as if Hubert were some kind of prehistoric monster. I will say for Miss Easter that she not only made Ronald take the posters down, but she also went on record as disapproving of the claims of the People's Party. But it was hard to understand what Miss Easter wanted. You could see why she was against posters which were not true, but she was just as much against a People's Party poster about Agatha's being born in a log cabin, which was true. Agatha's father has a cabin in northern Wisconsin, and Agatha was born there unexpectedly, which is just like Agatha. She's always turn-ing up when she's not expected. Hubert said that he could have got out an answering poster pointing out that unpreparedness runs in the Crawley family. But Miss Easter wouldn't let the People's Party use the log cabin poster. It didn't make sense. First, she wanted us to conduct our election like a national election, and then she got upset when we did. There was no pleasing Miss Easter. And, as usual, the more interested we got in the election, the more she began to act as if she wanted to forget the whole project.

The thing above all else that seemed to upset Miss Easter was the reappearance of Dino Sanders in school and his interest in Miss Easter's project. Dino is hardly ever in school between November and March. His mother says he's delicate. He's not delicate in the summertime. Dino lives in the country, and all summer, if you ride your bike in the direction of his farm, you can see him flying around all over the countryside on a swell pony as if he were carrying a message like "The British are coming." But he gets delicate in the winter because he hates school. He always manages to get promoted because he's smart. Also, the teachers can't stand having him around.

Anyway, in the nick of time when it looked as if nothing could keep Agatha from being elected, Dino decided to come to school for a while. He announced immediately that he was going to be a write-in candidate, and that he would solicit the vote of the Independents. This announcement changed the whole election picture. Nobody had known there were any Independents up to that point, but if Dino ran, there were sure to be some. The girls like him because he has curly hair and is funny. And the boys like him because he's crazy. Besides, Dino said he was going to run on a reform ticket and he had a million ideas for improving the school. It was the first break that the Other People's Party had had, for as Hubert said, Dino was a cinch to cut into Agatha's constituency. The only person, besides Ronald of course, who seemed to be against Dino's candidacy was Miss Easter, who was starting to take a negative view of everything. However, as Dino said, she couldn't keep him off the ticket, because after all this is a democracy.

Dino's platform had it all over Agatha's or even Hubert's. Agatha was running on a platform against dirt and disease and ignorance in the school, and she had plans to set up about a thousand committees: for example, a clean-up committee to wash blackboards and to inform on litterbugs; a discipline committee to set up playground rules and sit on a board and penalize everybody who broke the rules; an educational committee to teach the little kids to play orderly games instead of just running around squawking. She had a lot of other dull ideas.

Hubert, in his first speech, had pointed out that Agatha's plan to have us do the janitors' and teachers' work wasn't reasonable, since we didn't get paid for it and they did. And he also pointed out that Agatha's ideas about discipline committees and informers were the first step toward a police state. He said that Agatha had been allowed to run and squawk when she was in the first grade and he thought that little kids should have a right to run and squawk without interference from the fifth grade government. But Miss Easter interrupted Hubert's speech to ask what *he* proposed to do to improve the class and the school. So in his second speech Hubert said that he was for freedom and democracy and against foreign interference. He told me later that he took several of his lines out of speeches by Presidential candidates, which explained the part about labor and management. But although Miss Easter didn't interrupt him the second time, she sighed a lot. You could tell that she was prejudiced against Hubert.

But then she was even against Dino's platform, which had something in it for everybody and which he posted on the bulletin board the first day he came back to school. I don't remember all of Dino's ideas, but here are some of them: nobody goes to school unless he wants to; everybody studies only what he wants to study because he knows better than anyone else what he likes and needs; ice cream breaks every hour; better school lunches or at least bigger portions; longer recesses; more recesses; no paddling; two baseball mitts in every locker; rewards for everybody with good marks; rewards for everybody with bad marks, so nobody will get a complex; rewards for everybody else because this is a democracy.

But Miss Easter gave a speech about individualism and democracy and order versus anarchy and disorder. She said that Dino was missing the point and asked him how he proposed to put his ideas into operation. But when Dino said that he had some great methods in mind and wanted to give a speech about them, Miss Easter decided that there wasn't any more time for speeches. As Dino said, she wouldn't give him equal time with the other candidates, and this was supposed to be a democracy.

So when the day came for voting, there was a lot of sympathy for Dino because he had been denied his rights. Besides, he had announced that if he won, he would give a party and invite everybody who voted for him.

Chapter XXIX
TROUBLE AT THE POLLS

Right before recess on election day, Miss Easter gave another speech. She said that it was important that we take an intelligent interest in government because we all had a stake in the future and if we hoped to get what we wanted and have good government, we must consider seriously a candidate's merits and fitness and plans, and exercise judgment and reason. Then she bawled Dino out for whispering. Then she told us about the voting machines which we didn't have and how they worked. Then she bawled out Dino, who seemed to be worried about something and who was still whispering to everybody. Then she gave another talk about responsible citizenship and our stake in the future. Then she told Dino that his immediate future included staying in during recess for whispering. Then she passed out ballots and after we'd checked our choice, she went around with the ballot box and we registered our votes. Since there wasn't time to count the votes before recess, she had Willie carry the ballot box into a little room off the classroom until after recess when the counting committee was going to tabulate the votes.

During recess there was a lot of predicting about the outcome of the election. Agatha, who had started using a lot of big political terms because Hubert did, said that she had unfounded confidence in the people and predicted that the people had supported her because she offered them government instead of anarchy. Ronald predicted that the People's Party would win because Miss Easter was on Agatha's side. Hubert predicted that he wouldn't care if he lost, so long as Agatha lost, too. Dino was unpredictable because he was staying in for whispering. Then Morris reported that what Dino kept whispering to everybody in the back of the room was not to vote for him. We couldn't understand Dino's making a switch like this when he'd been so bent on winning. But whatever the reason, the news really shook Hubert, because if enough people had heard Dino, Agatha might have recovered some supporters. Hubert said that now the fate of the nation was hanging in the balance.

When we returned to class after recess, even those people who didn't know about the fate of the nation were all worked up over the outcome of the election. So right away Miss Easter sent Ronald in to get the ballot box. She was giving us instructions about some assignments for the next day, and she didn't notice at first that Ronald was taking a long time getting the box. But I did, and it made me suspicious. You never know what Ronald Pruitt might be up to. Well, Ronald didn't come back and he didn't come back, and finally Miss Easter went to see what was keeping him. She met him coming, and he explained that he couldn't find the box anywhere. Miss Easter said that the box had to be there. She asked Willie where he'd set it. and Willie said on the table in the middle of the room. But it wasn't on the table. Miss Easter looked everywhere in the little room, and then she looked everywhere in the classroom, too. She looked in all the cupboards and waste-baskets and everywhere. But the ballot box had disap-peared.

"Well, isn't that strange?" said Miss Easter when she finally stopped looking. "A big box like that. What could have become of it?"

At this, Ronald made a big thing of turning around in his seat and shaking his head and looking back at Dino. Immediately, Dino, who'd been looking a lot less worried since the disappearance of the ballot box, leaped to his feet.

"I am under suspicion," he yelled in this way he has that drives the teachers crazy. "I demand to be searched."

"Be quiet, Dino," said Miss Easter. "Stop dramatizing yourself. Why should anyone suspect you?"

It was a dumb question. Miss Easter herself was get-ting this suspicious look in her eye. Teachers always find it easy to suspect Dino.

"Ask Ronald," said Dino. "He's wobbling his head at me."

Miss Easter said that after we'd spent a week and a half on the subject of the importance of responsible, intelligent, informed, honest voters, she was sure that no one in the fifth grade had had anything to do with the dis-appearance of the ballot box. But she didn't sound sure. And Agatha suggested that since Dino had spent only three days on the subject, maybe he had done something with the ballot box during recess when he was alone in the room.

"Where would I put it?" yelled Dino, taking this chance to jump up and dance around in the aisle. "I demand my constitutional rights. I demand a lawyer. I demand to be searched. I demand that my desk be searched. I demand that the room be searched again. I demand that everybody be searched."

Dino told me later that it was the best time he'd ever had in school, and he made such a racket that finally Miss Easter searched him and his desk to shut him up. But she didn't find the votes, and the box was too big to put into a desk, anyway.

"Ronald says that Dino probably carried the box out during recess when no one was looking," said Agatha, as Miss Easter completed her search of Dino's desk.

Miss Easter put her hand over Dino's mouth and held him down in his seat while she explained that she'd been on hall duty right outside the classroom all during recess and that Dino had not left the room. It had occurred to me that Ronald was making a big point of throwing suspicion on Dino. Of course, Ronald just naturally likes to see other people in trouble, but it seemed to me that he might have a special reason. I was remembering with my trained detective brain that Ronald also had had motive and opportunity.

"I think that Ronald ought to be searched, too," I said. "He was in that room alone a long time."

Immediately, most of the kids, expecially the Other People's Party, turned their suspicions from Dino to Ronald and began insisting that Miss Easter search him.

Miss Easter, who was looking quite bothered and hot, said, "I think that this discussion has gone far enough. We'll probably learn that the box was carried away by accident. So we'll turn to our arithmetic lesson and look for the ballot box later."

But obviously this wouldn't do. Practically everybody thought that Ronald ought to be searched.

"All the suspects should have equal treatment," said Dino, dancing around. "I insist on it as a responsible citizen."

"Search me," said Ronald, surprising everybody. "I want to be searched."

And finally Miss Easter searched him and his desk, but she didn't find the votes.

"Even if I did have the votes, which I don't, what would I do with the box?" said Ronald. "Anyway, how about Willie? He was the last person seen with the box. Maybe he didn't even set it on the table."

"I did, too, you big troublemaker," said Willie.

At this point, Miss Easter got tough. The room was in an uproar. Some of the people in class suspected Dino, and some suspected Ronald, and one or two even suspected Willie, although everybody knows that Willie always tells the truth.

"We will settle the matter of these accusations once and for all," said Miss Easter. "Now I'm going to put you boys on your honor to answer my questions truthfully and exactly. Willie, did you set the box on the table, as you said you did?"

"Yes, I absolutely did," said Willie.

"Dino, did you remove the box from the room?"

"I absolutely did not," said Dino.

"Ronald, did you do anything with the box?"

"No," said Ronald.

"Willie, do you know where the votes are?"

"As far as I know, they're in thin air," said Willie.

"Do you know where they are, Dino?"

"As far as I know, they're at the bottom of the sea," said Dino in a joyful tone.

"Ronald, do you know where they are?"

"No," said Ronald.

"He isn't answering as exactly as Willie and Dino are," said Morris.

"That's enough," said Miss Easter. "We'll have no more accusations. We'll probably discover a perfectly simple explanation for the disappearance of the box. Perhaps one of the janitors carried it away."

"How could that happen if you were by the door?" said Dino. "Anyway, you were the only person I saw in class during recess."

But Miss Easter said that she trusted that everybody in the room was satisfied now and that probably by afternoon the box would be found and that, in the meantime, we'd turn to our lesson. Well, I wasn't satisfied. I still suspected Ronald, and just before we were dismissed for lunch, I got an idea. As soon as the bell rang, I went and looked out of the window in the little room to see whether Ronald had dropped the box out of the window. But there was nothing there.

At lunch the fifth grade class members couldn't talk about anything but the mystery.

"If anybody can get to the bottom of this, Andy and Willie can," Freddie Clark told everybody.

But for the first time since we'd gone into the detective business, I wasn't optimistic. For one thing, I was used to working with Willie. But since apparently Willie couldn't concentrate on anything at this point except baseball, it was obvious that I was going to have to tackle the case all by myself.

Chapter XXX
A STAKE IN THE FUTURE

A detective concentrates on motive and opportunity. So after lunch I went back to the classroom and all by myself started thinking. Hubert and Agatha had motive to get hold of the box and stuff it, but no opportunity. Besides, Miss Easter had told us that stuffing a ballot box was dishonest. Agatha may be only a girl, but if there's one thing about Agatha Crawley, she's honest. So is Hubert. So I drew a line through them. Willie had opportunity, but Willie wouldn't be dishonest and stuff a ballot box, either. So I eliminated Willie. Dino, Ronald, and Miss Easter had both opportunity and motive. And Dino might stuff it. He'd reported at lunch that when his mother heard about the party Dino was going to give if he was elected, she had said that Dino was one politician who could not dip his hand into her purse and call it concern for the general welfare and that the party would be paid for out of Dino's allowance. So Dino, who had the best chance to win, didn't want to win. Ronald would definitely stuff any ballot box. And Ronald would do anything to show me up as campaign manager. Miss Easter was an unknown quantity. I never could figure out the way her mind worked. But everybody knew that she was against the Independents and the Other People. So I made red circles around Dino, Ronald, and Miss Easter.

Then I considered the method of the crime. On Ronald I drew a blank. But Dino could have carried the box out of the room, because Miss Easter could have alibied him for unknown reasons. Or Miss Easter could have sneaked it out when Dino wasn't looking. So I made blue stars around Dino and Miss Easter. At this point I heard a noise and looked up to see this small first grader wandering around. He was just coming out of the little room. Little kids do funny things. Once during recess a first grader went to sleep in the enclosed part below Miss Easter's desk. Nobody knew he was there, and when he woke up and put these small fingers on Miss Easter's leg to pull himself out, everybody thought that Miss Easter had gone into convulsions right in the middle of geography. Being way below eye level, all the little children in school had opportunity, and being peculiar, they didn't need motive. It was a tough mystery running over with suspects. I finally decided that for the time being I'd better play catch and give my brain a rest. Miss Easter had said that the box would be found by afternoon, and if I could see who it had been stuffed for, maybe I could identify the box-taker.

But when the afternoon bell rang for classes, Miss Easter had to admit that the box was still missing.

"If it is never found," said Agatha, "how are we to know who is supposed to improve the school?"

Miss Easter, who seemed a lot less interested in this point than she had been, said, "The box will probably be found by tomorrow morning. We'll just wait and see."

But that's what she'd said about the afternoon. You can't just keep waiting. All the kids said so. And as Hubert told me privately, how could we sleep that night with the fate of the nation hanging in the balance. Several people who had been discussing the matter during the noon period when I was busy deducting, said why didn't we nominate the candidates again and vote by a show of hands the way we had always done before we learned to be reasonable. Everybody was in favor of this, and finally Miss Easter said we could.

So we started all over.

"I nominate Agatha," said Betsy.

"Second the nomination," said Ronald.

"I nominate Hubert," said Freddie.

"Second the nomination," I said.

"I withdraw my candidacy for financial reasons," said Dino.

You can imagine how the Other People felt when this happened. Hubert and Morris looked as if they were in an earthquake. Then at this crucial point, Willie started showing an interest at last. You can always count on Willie.

"I think that there should be a third candidate so there'll be a choice," said Willie. "And I've thought of a candidate who has merit and fitness and plans. I nominate Archie Monroe."

"Second the nomination," said Morris and Hubert.

Well, you never could figure Miss Easter. We had been sure that she was for Agatha, and we knew by experience that she hardly ever agrees with Willie. But for the first time since the first days of the project, she looked pleased. And with Archie being popular and not having bored the class with dull speeches and with the other candidates under suspicion because of the missing ballot box, the outcome was obvious. Archie was elected almost unanimously.

It turned out to be the best choice we could have made. At first, Archie wasn't very enthusiastic, because he said that he'd drawn a long straw and wasn't supposed to run. But then he began to get ideas about improving the school, and he got interested in the job. For example, he put Ronald and all the girls on committees taking care of the little kids so that Ronald and the girls wouldn't be always getting in our way on the playground. Ronald was furious because he was put with the girls. Archie turned out to be such a good president that if he ever runs for President of the United States, he'll get the vote of everybody in our class, except Ronald. Every time Ronald caused trouble or was mean to somebody, Archie figured out a lousy new job for Ronald. Archie's clamping down on Ronald that way improved the school and made life pleasanter for everybody. And Agatha Crawley says that she'll never run for President as long as a man as capable as Archie is available.

170

But the box never did turn up. In a few days everybody else forgot about it, but the problem kept bothering me because I'm a detective. I tried to work on the angle of who gained. Archie and Hubert gained, but they didn't have opportunity. Dino, who did have opportunity, also gained. But then I realized that with Archie as president, Miss Easter and everybody in the fifth grade gained, except maybe Ronald. It seemed to me, though, that the best suspects were Miss Easter and Dino. But I couldn't see any way of figuring out which one had taken the box.

Then when I had practically given up ever solving the case, one day on the baseball field the answer suddenly hit me right between the pitcher's box and the bench. Willie had just made a phenomenal catch at first base which retired the side.

"I guess nobody runs rings around me at first base," said Willie to Archie, who was slapping him on the back.

"Not as long as you make catches like that," said Archie, who was Willie's second best friend.

I don't know why I hadn't figured it out sooner. However, as Willie said later, it was an extra-tough mystery if he did say so. The tricky part was that when Willie, who always tells the truth, is told to answer *exactly*, he does. If he said that he set the box on the table, he did. And if he said that as far as he knew the votes were in thin air, they were. But that didn't mean that he didn't drop the box out of the window after he set it on the table and that he didn't take it down to the furnace room during recess and burn the votes. What gave me the clue was suddenly realizing that there was Willie, a big gainer, on first base, because after Willie had nominated Archie to a job which Archie turned out to like, Archie didn't have the heart to take first base away from Willie.

Willie was as pleased as Punch that I had finally solved the case. And he lost no time in letting all our best friends know what a great detective I was and what a responsible citizen he was.

"That's what I call downright patriotism," said Hubert, "and using your brain besides."

"Where's the patriotism?" said Archie. "He was thinking about first base."

"For Pete's sake, Archie, what do you think I am—a creep?" said Willie. "Do you think that even if Agatha's mother were baseball coach, I'd back Agatha and risk the future of the country? Both of you guys are wrong. I wasn't thinking of one thing. I was thinking of everything. You're forgetting that Miss Easter told us to exercise our reason and think of everything. And you're especially forgetting Miss Easter's last speech about taking an interest in government because of a stake in the future. I will admit that at first while she was talking, all I thought of was the future baseball season, which made me wish that Archie would be too busy being president to try for first base. But then the wish made me think how much better president a smart person like Archie would make than Agatha, who is only a girl, or Dino, who is crazy, or Hubert, who was getting so political he was losing his reason."

"I was only trying to save the country," said Hubert.

"That's no excuse," said Willie. "So besides thinking of my baseball future, I was thinking of the future of the United States if Agatha won and the future of the class if any of the candidates won. And after I set the box on the table, it came to me in a flash that no one else had as many futures in mind as I had or was considering a candidate on the basis of so many reasons and that if Miss Easter was right about reasonable citizens accepting responsibility so that mistakes could be avoided, then it was my duty to do what I could. So I got philosophic and dropped the box out of the window."

We all agreed that obviously Willie was thinking of more futures than anyone else and being more reasonable and responsible, to say nothing of more philosophic. As Freddie pointed out, "Logic is logic." But Willie, who said that in order to give me time to demonstrate my detective genius, he had already put off too long getting the fame and praise that were coming to him, was bent on telling Miss Easter right away. And there was a chance that Miss Easter with all her prejudice and bad logic wouldn't admit that Willie, who had thought of the most stakes in the future, had learned the most from her project. You have to learn to be cautious around grown-ups like Miss Easter, who has a bad habit of looking for a dark side. So Archie and I talked Willie into telling Mr. Barrie first.

It's a good thing he did. Mr. Barrie said that he would advise Willie to forego the fame. He said that even though *he* could believe that, as Hubert kept saying, all that running up and down stairs burning votes showed a lot of public spirit, he was convinced that Miss Easter would not see it as proof of the success of her project, since vote-burning is wrong.

"Even when you are giving the democratic process a chance?" said Willie.

"Even then," said Mr. Barrie, blowing his nose. I've decided that Mr. Barrie is allergic to Willie, because lately every time he talks to Willie his eyes water and he does a lot of nose-blowing.

"Why would Miss Easter overlook such a crucial point?" said Willie. "She never said one single word against giving people an opportunity to vote again."

"She probably didn't foresee that the question would come up," said Mr. Barrie.

"Well, it's very confusing," said Willie. "But I think I'm getting the idea. Now even though Miss Easter has taught me to be reasonable and responsible, I'm to do my best to let other people make mistakes."

Mr. Barrie wiped his eyes. "The democratic process is a complicated matter to sort out right now during recess," he said. "But if you'll come in to see me some day after school, we'll talk it over."

"We know all there is to know now, don't we?" said Hubert as we went out to the playground. "What does he want to talk about?"

"Search me," said Willie. "But he knows I saved the country, even though I did it in the wrong way. So he's probably going to try to talk me into being a Congressman when I grow up."

Since we knew from experience that Miss Easter would focus on Willie's wrongdoing instead of on his good intentions, we all took the Dreadful Loyal Oath not to tell. Anyone who breaks the Dreadful Loyal Oath gets rabies, but since I administered it, I forgot to take it. And now that Agatha has given up her political ambitions and Miss Easter has recently passed us all out of the fifth grade, all the guys agree that it is now all right for me to reveal the truth.

So that's the true story of how Willie saved the day when the fate of the nation was hanging in the balance, and got to be first baseman besides.

Chapter XXXI

TIME TO TAKE A BREATHER

Last fall when Mr. Barrie gave me a book of Sherlock Holmes's cases to read and then kept supplying me with more and talking with me about them, Ronald Pruitt got jealous. So he kept saying to everybody wasn't it a shame and a pity that an account of Willie's and my cases wasn't available because he was dying to read a really good book. You'd think that after Ronald had said something about a million times, even he would get tired of it, but Ronald never gets tired. He started this wisecracking in September, and he was still on the subject in January. So finally one day I told Ronald that I *was* going to put down an account of Willie's and my cases and get famous. Having his wisecracks backfire like this squelched Ronald for about three days, but then he started all over again, this time on how much longer was he going to have to wait for me to be famous, which is one reason I've stuck to the job.

Already I've got a little fame. Late in February when

Mr. Barrie went skiing and then had to lie in the hospital for several weeks with his leg in the air, he asked me to mail him my account of each case as soon as I'd written it down, and so Mr. Reagan, the postmaster, already calls me the young author. Mr. Barrie told me later that he credited me as much as the doctor with the fact that he got back to school in record time. When I told Mr. McCotter that my writing had helped to fix up Mr. Barrie's bone, Mr. McCotter said he wasn't surprised. He said that the written word can be a powerful medicine and that one reason he reads a chapter of the Bible every night before he goes to bed is that he is convinced it will help him to wake up in good health in this world or the next. Besides, Mr. McCotter says that there was a hunter in Montana who dislocated his collar bone a hundred miles from a doctor, and happening to have a book of poetry with him, he read a poem aloud to himself and his collar bone just naturally backed into place. Mr. McCotter says it was a famous case which annoyed the entire medical profession.

I'm glad I was able to help Mr. Barrie out, but if I had known how much trouble making a book was going to be, I'd probably never have started. And if it hadn't been for Mr. McCotter, I probably wouldn't have stuck to it, in spite of Ronald's wisecracks. But Mr. McCotter says that once you start doing something worthwhile, you have to finish it. He says that this is one of his strongest principles and the main reason he hasn't started many projects himself because if a man doesn't live up to his principles, he might as well shoot himself. So I stuck to it, and now Mr. McCotter has advised me that it's time to take a breather. He says being famous isn't everything.

I've been a little worried, anyway, that all this think-ing and sitting would stunt my growth. Morris Somers, who has measured my height and muscles before and after I put down each case, says that his records don't show any evidence of stunting yet. So after I take a breather, I may even start again and put down an account of Willie's and my two recent cases—the fantastic case of the unidentified flying object and the peculiar case of Mr. McCotter's missing boat—and all the other cases Willie and I are sure to have during this summer vacation coming up. But if it turns out that I've suffered some ill effects, I'll drop the whole idea. I'd rather be big than famous.

The main reason I'd even consider making another book is my father, who gave me the surprise of my life today. I've always wanted to impress my father, but he's hard to impress and as the foregoing events have shown, he's never been in favor of my going into the detec-tive business. Besides, my father is a born critic. You should have heard him this morning at breakfast. He and my mother watched a certain conversation television pro-gram last night, and this morning he said that somebody who said that the age of the common man was in danger of becoming the age of the common denominator was right. I wrote this down at the time in case it should ever come in handy against Ronald Pruitt, because if a common denominator is bad, then Ronald is a common denom-inator if I ever saw one. My father said that one evening with those twentieth-century refugees from an empty head, an over-active thyroid, and an appetite for the sound of applause had given him a seventeenth-century malady known as the griping of the guts. My mother said she saw no need for him to bring up the seventeenth century, and my father said what he was bringing up was the twentieth, because he had no stomach for a mixture of platitude and prurience. He said that when people with an overriding respect for the cut of a vest could conceive of themselves as voices crying in the wilderness, then it was time for all good men to take to the woods with booby traps or die laughing. My mother told him not to act superior and intolerant, and my father said it wasn't an act. It was a noisy breakfast, and my father's disposition didn't improve, even though today is Sunday. This afternoon he started reading a best seller, which ended up being thrown clear across the room into the wastebasket. Finally, he said he was going to shut himself up in his study with Dr. Samuel Johnson, which was a relief to everybody because Dr. Johnson always has a good effect on my father's disposition. Dr. Samuel Johnson is a famous man who has been dead for a long time.

You can imagine how I felt when I came home late in the afternoon and found that I'd forgot and left my account of Willie's and my cases on my father's desk when I was checking a word in his dictionary and Willie and Archie came in to ask me to come out. And you can imaging my surprise when my father came to the dinner table in a good mood. He told me that he was impressed, especially with my persistence. I said I probably wouldn't have stuck to it if it hadn't been for Ronald Pruitt and Mr. McCotter, and my father said that perhaps he'd been wrong this morning, that as Willie would say, the world needs creeps and humbugs. I never heard Willie say any such thing, but I wasn't going to point this out to my father when he was in such a good mood. So today has turned out to be one of my best days. I'd rather impress my father than be famous.

So that's all of Willie's and my cases for the time being while I take a breather. Tomorrow morning Willie and I are going fishing because Mr. McCotter says that the suckers are biting. Besides, a suspicious, bearded stranger with long hair has rented the old cabin on Walnut Fork. Willie, who had a conversation with the stranger, says that he drives a foreign car—a used Sunbeam. He goes around looking up in the air with binoculars, and he told Willie that he was a bird watcher, but Willie thinks that he is a foreign spy and that a carrier pigeon is coming in with messages. So we are going to fish off the sandy bank right below the cabin, and so that we can kill two birds with one stone, we're going to take our slingshots as well as our fishing rods. From now on we're going to keep an eye on that bird watcher. Any spy who comes to Wakanda had better be careful what he does with Willie and me around, because we have a whole summer in front of us with nothing to do but be on the lookout for spies.